Penguin Study Notes

KT-447-979

JANE AUSTIN
Pride and Prejudice

SUSAN QUILLIAM, M.A.
Advisory Editor: STEPHEN COOTE, M.A., PH.D.

PENGUIN BOOKS

PENGUIN BOOKS

Published by the Penguin Group
Penguin Books Ltd, 27 Wrights Lane, London w8 5tz, England
Penguin Putnam Inc., 375 Hudson Street, New York, New York 10014, USA
Penguin Books Australia Ltd, Ringwood, Victoria, Australia
Penguin Books Canada Ltd, 10 Alcorn Avenue, Toronto, Ontario, Canada m4v 3b2
Penguin Books (NZ) Ltd, Private Bag 102902, NSMC, Auckland, New Zealand

Penguin Books Ltd, Registered Offices: Harmondsworth, Middlesex, England

First published in Penguin Passnotes 1984
Published in Penguin Study Notes 1999
10 9 8 7 6 5 4 3 2

Copyright © Susan Quillam, 1984
All rights reserved

Set in 10/12.5pt PostScript Monotype Ehrhardt
Typeset by Rowland Phototypesetting Ltd, Bury St Edmunds, Suffolk
Printed in England by Clays Ltd, St Ives plc

Except in the United States of America, this book is sold subject
to the condition that it shall not, by way of trade or otherwise, be lent,
re-sold, hired out, or otherwise circulated without the publisher's
prior consent in any form of binding or cover other than that in
which it is published and without a similar condition including this
condition being imposed on the subsequent purchaser

HAMPSHIRE COUNTY LIBRARY

823
AUS

040772820

C003858216

Contents

To the Student

This book is designed to help you with your studies and examinations. It contains a synopsis of the plot, a glossary of the more unfamiliar words and phrases, and a commentary on some of the issues raised by the text. An account of the writer's life is also included for background.

Page references in parentheses refer to the Penguin Classics edition, edited by Vivien Jones. Chapter numbers follow those that appear in a continuously numbered sequence at the top of each right-hand page of this edition.

When you use this book, remember that it is no more than an aid to your study. It will help you find passages quickly and perhaps give you ideas for essays. But remember: *This book is not a substitute for reading the text and it is your knowledge and your response that matter.* These are the things the examiners are looking for and they are also the things that will give you the most pleasure. Show your knowledge and appreciation to the examiner, and show them clearly.

Introduction

The Life and Background of Jane Austen (1775–1817)

Jane Austen's novels are very different from those of our own age, and so it can sometimes be difficult to appreciate them. One way to break down the barriers and begin to understand her novels is to look at how Jane Austen herself lived. Her novels spring directly from her own experience and the issues she deals with in *Pride and Prejudice* are those which directly concerned her in her day.

Jane Austen was born in 1775 in an England that was changing in almost every way. The French Revolution and the rise of Napoleon were imminent, about to turn upside down most people's ideas of social stability and the class system. Agricultural Britain was fast changing into industrial Britain, with all the problems and poverty that involved. The staid, traditional religions were being threatened by non-conformist Methodism, and the regulated Classical art and literature of the time were giving way to emotional Romanticism.

None of these events, which were to alter England so radically in the coming years, really touched families of Jane Austen's sort. Upper middle class, professional, conservative, her family lived in a quiet part of rural Hampshire. Her father was a country rector, her six brothers and one sister, Cassandra, grew up in the rectory at Steventon. From what we know, they were a happy family, lively and educated. Jane and her sister went to school in Oxford and Reading, then came back to the family circle. From the age of nine Jane never left her family, and although they moved when their father retired to Bath in 1801, they returned to Hampshire after his death, living first in Southampton then Chawton.

Jane's life focused on the small, closed communities of upper-middle-class people in the places where she lived. She, as her heroines do, made morning visits, gave dinners and attended balls with the same circle of friends. To us this may seem a boring existence, but remember that to Jane Austen it was perfectly normal, secure and happy. She, like Elizabeth, surely found her fulfilment in being 'a studier of character' who realized that 'people themselves alter so much, that there is something new to be observed in them for ever' (p. 38).

For a woman such as Jane Austen, marriage was the most obvious aim in life. So the meeting of men, the mutual assessment of suitability, courtship and marriage must have been important to her, and as we know these are key topics in her novels. In fact, with the sensitivity and sensibility of her own heroines, Jane Austen herself did not rush into any financially sound but emotionally unworthy marriage. There was a romance – we do not know the young man's name – which was on the point of an engagement when he was killed in a tragic accident. Later in life, a close friend, Harris Bigg-Wither, proposed to Jane and she accepted; but by the next morning she had faced the fact that she did not love him, and broke off the engagement. Neither she nor her sister Cassandra ever married.

Jane Austen was by no means the despised spinster. She was close to, and loved by, her sister, brothers, nephews and nieces. Also, she found fulfilment in her work. She began writing early in life, and we have every reason to believe her family supported her fully, though at first her work met with little success. Her father sent her first novel, *First Impressions* – the lost original of *Pride and Prejudice* – to a publisher as soon as it was finished, offering to pay for the printing himself. It was rejected and Jane Austen laid it aside to begin work on *Sense and Sensibility*. This too was left for some years until she revised and published it in 1811. It was successful enough for her to return to *First Impressions*, to rewrite it and present it in 1813 as *Pride and Prejudice*. From the start, this seemed her most popular novel: it quickly reprinted. *Mansfield Park* was published in 1814, *Emma* in 1816, and *Northanger Abbey* and *Persuasion* were published posthumously in 1818. *Lady Susan* and a fragment, *The Watsons*, were included in a memoir of Jane

Austen's life in 1871 and her adolescent writings and an unfinished novel, *Sanditon*, were published in the twentieth century.

Hardly touched by success, Jane Austen remained with her family throughout her life, and even hid scraps of her writing when visitors or servants entered a room in which she was working. None of her novels brought her great financial reward, but even after the death of her father she escaped spinsterly poverty; the family was cared for by her brothers.

Jane Austen died tragically early. She contracted tuberculosis and, despite moving to Winchester for better medical attention, she died in 1817. She is buried in Winchester Cathedral.

How far do Jane Austen's novels reflect her life? The answer is, almost entirely. She writes about what she knows – upper-middle-class communities containing parsons, soldiers, minor aristocracy; houses much like those she lived in; assemblies like those she must have attended at Bath; visits to relations; trips to Brighton and London. She writes of the things in life that were important to her and her society – family life, meetings, courtship, marriage, the relationships that make up any community.

It is very noticeable that Jane Austen's books do not reflect the more radical events of the times in which she lived. She mentions war briefly in *Pride and Prejudice*, but only as a device for introducing Wickham. She has Elizabeth visit Pemberley, but states firmly that 'it is not the object of this work to give a description of Derbyshire' (p. 197). Neither does she follow the literary fashion of the time. She keeps to the ideas and style of the Classical tradition and to its sound values and to a rational approach to life, although it was a view fast giving way to a more emotional approach, even at the time Jane Austen was writing.

It is tempting to think of Jane Austen's work as being out of touch with life and irrelevant to everyday concerns. But the very fact that she avoids detailed contemporary references makes her more relevant, even timeless. She knew that for most people of her generation, war and revolution were things they heard about but that did not seem directly to touch their lives. Far more important, to them and to us, were the universal events on which society is founded even now – love, attraction, marriage, emotions, jealousy and sexuality.

Try to see, then, that *Pride and Prejudice* is a novel that came directly from Jane Austen's own experiences, and that it has a real meaning for all readers, in whatever situation and whatever time they may be.

Synopsis of Pride and Prejudice

The prime objective of Mrs Bennet, wife of Mr Bennet of Longbourn, is to marry off her five daughters, Jane, Elizabeth, Mary, Lydia and Kitty. The arrival of Mr Bingley, a rich bachelor, to nearby Netherfield Park therefore causes great excitement.

The Bennets' first real view of Bingley is at an assembly (pp. 12–14) at Meryton which he attends with his two sisters, brother-in-law, and friend, Darcy. Bingley is obviously attracted to Jane, though Darcy, despite being rich and handsome, is disliked by everyone (p. 12); he seems unimpressed by the assembly and Elizabeth overhears him slighting her (p. 13).

Jane tells Elizabeth that she admires Bingley (p. 15), and though Elizabeth mistrusts the Bingley sisters, the friendship between them and Jane develops (p. 21). Jane is not demonstrative, however, and Elizabeth's friend Charlotte Lucas warns her that Jane should show Bingley her feelings or risk losing him (p. 21). Elizabeth, meanwhile, is unaware that she has attracted Darcy's interest (p. 23). During a gathering at the Lucas home, her forthright manner attracts him even more: this makes Bingley's sister, Caroline, jealous as she wants Darcy for herself (p. 26).

Jane rides over to dine at Netherfield (p. 29), catches a chill and has to stay – much to the delight of Mrs Bennet who sees a chance of furthering the connection with Bingley. Elizabeth goes to look after Jane (pp. 30–31) until she is well enough to return home five days later (p. 53).

This period, while strengthening Jane and Bingley's friendship, also reveals the Bingley sisters' disdain for the Bennets, particularly when Mrs Bennet visits Jane and embarrasses everyone by her behaviour (pp. 37–41).

Elizabeth and Darcy discover more about each other during her stay (pp. 35–6, 42–7, 49–51). She thinks him disagreeable but enjoys teasing him, while his admiration for her only increases. Eventually, afraid of raising her hopes – for he cannot imagine marrying into a family inferior to his own – he deliberately hides his feelings (pp. 52–3). But already Caroline Bingley's jealousy has increased (pp. 34–5, 42, 46–7, 48–51) and she repeatedly tries to win Darcy's favour and change his feelings for Elizabeth.

The day after the sisters' return to Longbourn, a visitor arrives. He is Mr Collins, a distant relative (p. 54); there being no son, the family estate will pass to him on Mr Bennet's death. Collins proves to be a self-centred and obsequious clergyman whose main preoccupation is his rich patroness, Lady Catherine de Bourgh (p. 58). Nevertheless, Mrs Bennet approves of him, for he too wants a wife (p. 61). Learning that Jane may soon be engaged, he turns his interest to Elizabeth (p. 62).

Next day, Mr Collins accompanies the sisters to visit their aunt, Mrs Philips, in Meryton. The younger girls also hope to see some of the officers whose regiment has recently been stationed there. While they are talking with a newly arrived officer named Wickham, Bingley and Darcy ride up and Elizabeth is aware of both recognition and embarrassment in the meeting between Darcy and Wickham (p. 63).

She learns the reason for this at a supper organized by Mrs Phillips when she talks to Wickham, whom she finds charming (p. 66). He tells her that Darcy's father had made provision in his will for Wickham, his steward's son, to have a church living, but that Darcy refused to grant it (pp. 68–9). Wickham speaks harshly of Darcy and his sister, adding that Lady Catherine, who is in fact Darcy's aunt, hopes that Darcy will marry her daughter Anne.

Bingley holds a ball at Netherfield; Elizabeth is disappointed that Wickham is not there to rescue her from Collins's continuing attentions (p. 76). Darcy is present, however, and she accepts his invitation to dance, although she finds him so disagreeable (p. 77). Despite Caroline Bingley's insistence on Darcy's innocence, Elizabeth believes Wickham's accusations (p. 81). The evening ends in embarrassment for her because of the tactless behaviour of her relations, particularly Collins (pp. 82–6).

The day after the ball, the clergyman proposes to Elizabeth (p. 89). At first he discounts her refusals, and although Mrs Bennet tries to change her daughter's mind Elizabeth stands firm. Jane meanwhile receives a letter from Caroline. Their party has gone to London. Elizabeth is sure this is only a temporary absence, but warns Jane that Caroline's friendship is false. She wants Bingley to marry Darcy's sister so that she herself can more easily marry Darcy (p. 100).

Collins is now courting Charlotte Lucas, and this results in a speedy proposal (p. 102), gladly accepted by Charlotte and her family (p. 103). Elizabeth, however, is upset, knowing her friend is making a marriage of convenience (pp. 104–5, 107), and Mrs Bennet is annoyed both at the loss of the potential suitor and at the thought of Charlotte's one day living at Longbourn. During the wedding preparations, a letter arrives from Caroline. Jane learns that Bingley is not returning to Netherfield and tries to accept the implication that the relationship is over (pp. 113–17).

Elizabeth finds relief from these sad developments in Wickham's company (p. 117) and in the Christmas visit of Mrs Bennet's brother, Mr Gardiner, and his family (p. 118). Mrs Gardiner, a particular friend of Elizabeth's, advises her not to encourage Wickham, who has no money and is therefore not a suitable match (pp. 122–3).

After Charlotte's marriage, the couple return to the parsonage at Hunsford (p. 123). Jane has gone to London with Mrs Gardiner. Her attempts to re-establish friendship with the Bingleys fail (pp. 124–6). For Elizabeth, too, there is disappointment as Wickham turns his attention to a young heiress. Elizabeth is surprised at how unaffected she feels (p. 126).

At the end of March, Elizabeth visits Charlotte, stopping in London on the way; she sees Jane and is invited to visit the Lakes in the summer, with the Gardiners (p. 129). Reaching Hunsford, she finds Charlotte surprisingly settled in her new life (pp. 130–31); the weeks pass pleasantly, despite regular visits to nearby Rosings, home of Lady Catherine, who proves to be proud and patronizing (pp. 134–40).

Just before Easter, Darcy and his cousin, Colonel Fitzwilliam, visit their aunt (p. 142). They call at the parsonage, and when Elizabeth next visits Rosings she finds Colonel Fitzwilliam's conversation pleasant and almost begins to enjoy Darcy's company (pp. 143–6). She watches closely for any signs of his favouring Anne de Bourgh, but can find none. Lady Catherine, however, seems uneasy at Darcy's attention to Elizabeth. Darcy now seeks Elizabeth out, visiting her and walking with her, but Elizabeth laughs at Charlotte's suggestion that he admires her (p. 150).

One day, while out walking, Colonel Fitzwilliam tells Elizabeth that Darcy recently influenced a close friend against an inferior marriage (pp. 153–4). Elizabeth realizes that he is referring to Bingley and Jane. She is so upset at Darcy's interference that she does not go to Rosings that evening (p. 155).

It is then that Darcy calls and proposes to Elizabeth (p. 156). Her temper is roused not only by the knowledge of his treatment of Jane and Wickham (pp. 158–9), but also by his confession that he has had to overcome a strong reluctance against marrying a social inferior (p. 159). Elizabeth refuses Darcy and they part in anger.

Next day, Darcy hands Elizabeth a letter (p. 161) which explains that he discouraged Bingley's marriage not only because of the Bennets' inferiority but also because Jane's behaviour convinced him that she did not return Bingley's affection (p. 163). As for Wickham, knowing him to be unprincipled and unsuited to the Church, Darcy gave him money to begin another career. When Wickham took up the idea again, Darcy refused him the living (pp. 164–5). In revenge, Wickham planned an elopement with Darcy's sister which was only prevented at the last moment (p. 166).

Elizabeth's reaction to this letter is crucial (pp. 168–72). She admits she can be prejudiced in her judgement, and also begins to realize the true worth of both Darcy and Wickham.

Elizabeth sees neither Darcy nor Colonel Fitzwilliam again before they leave (p. 173). Soon after, with final visits to Rosings (pp. 173–5) and a surprisingly regretful parting from the Collinses (pp. 177–8), Elizabeth returns to London where Jane joins her for the journey to Longbourn (p. 179). Kitty and Lydia meet them on the way with news that the regiment is moving to Brighton (p. 180). In addition Wickham is unattached again, his heiress having left the district (p. 181).

Once home, Elizabeth soon tells Jane everything, except for Darcy's part in discouraging Bingley's affections (pp. 184–5). Kindheartedly, she decides not to make public Wickham's misdeeds (p. 186).

Lydia, meanwhile, is heartbroken about the regiment's departure, but the Colonel's wife invites her to accompany them to Brighton (p. 188). Elizabeth foresees problems, but even her father will not listen to her (p. 189). Elizabeth and Wickham say good-bye, and she hints that she now knows the truth (pp. 191–2). The regiment leaves and Lydia too goes to Brighton (pp. 192–3).

Elizabeth's trip with the Gardiners begins in mid July. The holiday has to be curtailed, so they visit Derbyshire instead of the Lakes (p. 196). While staying nearby they decide to visit Darcy's house, Pemberley; Elizabeth's initial misgivings are allayed by the news that Darcy will not be there (p. 197).

Elizabeth is impressed both by Pemberley (pp. 201–2) and the obvious affection Darcy's housekeeper has for her master (pp. 203–4). She also sees his portrait, which stirs her emotions surprisingly (p. 205). Then, while they are in the gardens, Darcy himself appears (p. 205), having arrived a day earlier than expected. He seems gentle, less proud. He greets Elizabeth and her relations with courtesy and next day brings his sister to see them (p. 212). Bingley too visits, and it seems obvious that he still admires Jane (p. 214). Elizabeth is overcome by the change in Darcy. She dares to hope he still cares for her (p. 216). Next day, Elizabeth's party visits Pemberley, another sign of Darcy's favour, despite the presence of Caroline Bingley, who again criticizes Elizabeth but is firmly rebuked by Darcy (pp. 218–20).

Very soon after this, Elizabeth receives two letters from Jane. One tells of Lydia's elopement with Wickham, presumably to Scotland to marry (p. 222). The second contains worse news; they have gone to London, probably not intending to marry. Both the colonel of the regiment and Mr Bennet have followed them there. Elizabeth is distraught. Darcy finds her in this state (p. 224) and she tells him the news (pp. 225–6). He seems disturbed and leaves almost immediately (p. 226). Elizabeth is convinced that he sees the elopement as final proof of her family's inferiority and so believes this must be the end of their relationship (p. 226).

The Gardiners and Elizabeth return to Longbourn (p. 229), discussing the affair on the way. Elizabeth particularly blames herself for not revealing Wickham's real character (p. 231). She meets varying reactions from her family (pp. 232ff.) and reads Lydia's parting note (p. 236). Mr Gardiner follows Mr Bennet to London, and the family waits for news, which arrives in a series of letters.

Mr Gardiner contacts Mr Bennet (p. 239), but at first there is no word save the Colonel's reports of Wickham's large gambling debts (p. 241). Mr Bennet returns home, leaving matters in Mr Gardiner's hands (p. 241). In the meantime, a letter has arrived from Collins condemning the elopement (p. 240).

Then Wickham and Lydia are found. Mr Gardiner writes that at first they did not intend to marry, but have agreed to do so on payment of a small allowance and inheritance to Lydia (p. 244). Mr Bennet believes that his brother-in-law has bribed Wickham to marry Lydia, and wonders how to repay him (p. 245). Elizabeth too is worried over the outcome of such a marriage (p. 245), but Mrs Bennet is delighted; she will now have one daughter wed, even though living in the North, where Wickham is to join the regular army (p. 252).

Lydia and Wickham are married and, despite Mr Bennet's displeasure, visit Longbourn (p. 254). Lydia, seemingly unconcerned by the disgrace, describes the wedding (pp. 256–7) and reveals that Darcy attended. Elizabeth immediately writes to Mrs Gardiner for news and learns (pp. 259–61) that Darcy himself found the couple and persuaded Wickham to marry by paying off his debts and giving him money. Darcy's stated reason was that he blamed himself for not publicizing Wickham's character for fear of damaging the family reputation.

Elizabeth's reaction to this news mixes hope that she was the cause of Darcy's actions, shame at her previous treatment of him, and regret that now marriage seems impossible (pp. 262–3).

Elizabeth and Wickham exchange a few final words, she showing for her part that she knows the truth but will accept him into the family for Lydia's sake. Soon after, the newly-weds leave for the North (p. 266).

News arrives that Bingley is returning to Netherfield (pp. 266–7). Jane insists she is unaffected (p. 267), but when Bingley pays a visit to Longbourn their mutual affection is obvious (pp. 268–72). He is accompanied by Darcy, who seems withdrawn. This upsets Elizabeth (p. 273). During a party at Longbourn, they have only a brief opportunity to speak (p. 275) and soon after he leaves for London (p. 277). Bingley continues to visit Longbourn (pp. 277–78) and proposes to Jane, to everyone's delight (pp. 279–82).

Soon after, Lady Catherine calls unexpectedly at Longbourn (p. 283). She has heard rumours that Darcy and Elizabeth may be engaged (p. 285) and because of her wish that Darcy marry her own daughter (p. 286) she demands that Elizabeth decline his offer. Lady Catherine reminds her that the Bennet family is socially inferior to Darcy's and is newly disgraced (pp. 287–8). Elizabeth refuses this demand and Lady Catherine departs angrily (p. 289). Elizabeth realizes that his aunt's opposition may influence Darcy against her and is also upset when her father, receiving a letter from Collins which hints at Darcy's favouring Elizabeth, scoffs at the idea (p. 292).

Darcy soon returns from London and visits Longbourn. When Elizabeth thanks him for arranging Lydia's marriage, he replies that it was done for her, and asks if her feelings towards him are still the same. When she tells him how changed they are, he repeats his proposal and they soon reach a perfect understanding (pp. 294–5).

Darcy explains that Lady Catherine told him of her visit to Longbourn. He realized then that if Elizabeth were still against marrying him, she would have said so. That she did not encouraged Darcy to hope again (p. 295). They discuss the first proposal and the letter (pp. 296–7). Darcy admits that for him the episode was a humbling one, the beginning of his self-knowledge (pp. 297–8) and Elizabeth sees it as marking the start of her affection for him. Darcy also explains that during his recent visits to Longbourn he realized how sincere Jane's feelings were for Bingley, and so encouraged him to propose (p. 298).

That evening Elizabeth confides in Jane, who is surprised and delighted (pp. 300–301). Next day, Darcy approaches Mr Bennet (p. 302) who, once he knows Elizabeth's true feelings, happily consents to their marriage (p. 304). Mrs Bennet is overjoyed now that three of her five daughters are safely settled (p. 305).

Elizabeth and Darcy are married and live at Pemberley (p. 310),

where Georgiana and Elizabeth become great friends (p. 312). Bingley
and Jane soon follow them to Derbyshire. Kitty spends a great deal of
time there, while Mary stays with her parents. Lydia and Wickham's
marriage proves as unfortunate as Elizabeth expected (p. 311). Caroline
Bingley swallows her resentment, and so, eventually, does Lady Catherine, while the Gardiners remain as firm friends as ever to Darcy and
Elizabeth.

An Account of the Plot

Chapter 1, *pp. 5–7*

Whenever a rich bachelor moves into an area, neighbouring families immediately assume he wants a wife, and see him as a future husband for one of their daughters. We meet the Bennets of Longbourn. Mrs Bennet's aim in life is to marry off her five daughters. She tells Mr Bennet that Bingley, a handsome bachelor with a fortune, is to rent the neighbouring estate of Netherfield Park and she wants Mr Bennet to visit the newcomer. Mr Bennet teases his wife by pretending that he has no intention of doing this, even for his favourite daughter, Elizabeth.

The first chapter of any book is vital. It should introduce us to the main themes and characters, and involve us in what is going to happen. This first chapter establishes a humorous atmosphere and introduces us immediately to the main theme of marriage, warns us through the Bennets' own partnership of the uncertainties of marriage, and mentions the heroine, Elizabeth. You might like to judge for yourself how far the chapter also gains your interest.

Chapter 2, *pp. 8–10*

Despite his teasing, Mr Bennet is in fact one of Bingley's first callers but, typically, he keeps his wife in suspense by not telling her until after the visit. He then has to leave the room to avoid her effusive gratitude. She and the girls spend the rest of the evening discussing Bingley.

This is another introductory chapter, establishing further the Bennets' poor marriage, building the atmosphere of upper-middle-class life, setting the scene for Bingley's arrival, and introducing us to the five Bennet girls.

Chapter 3, *pp. 11–14*

Apart from a fleeting glimpse of him during his return visit to Longbourn, the girls learn little about Bingley until a ball at Meryton. Here we meet Bingley himself, a handsome gentleman and 'romantic hero' whose approval of everything and everyone makes him well liked. He takes a particular fancy to Jane, dancing with her twice. Accompanying Bingley are his two sisters, the husband of one of them, and a friend, Mr Darcy, who at first impresses everyone because he is handsome, rich and single. However, he seems very proud, dances only with his friends, and does not mix with Meryton society, which promptly turns against him. In particular, he snubs Elizabeth Bennet. Bingley suggests Darcy dance with her and, no doubt realizing she can overhear, Darcy comments that she is 'not handsome enough to tempt *me*' (p. 13). Elizabeth, though offended, repeats the story lightheartedly to her friends. Returning to Longbourn at the end of the evening, Mrs Bennet explains to her husband, at too-great length, everything that has happened.

This is the first social meeting between Darcy and Elizabeth. From the very beginning, their pride and prejudice are established. Darcy is presented as conceited and disagreeable, and it is easy to see why Elizabeth dislikes him, and how her prejudice begins. Look though at the first description of Darcy: 'fine . . . handsome . . . noble' (p. 12), before public opinion (and Elizabeth) turn against him. This is the true Darcy; Jane Austen is here showing us clearly the errors that prejudice can produce. Other points to notice are Elizabeth's endearing ability to laugh at herself, Bingley's indiscriminate approval of everything, and the emphasis on man-catching, built up through the girls' interest in Bingley and Mrs Bennet's comments at the end of the chapter.

Chapter 4, *pp. 15–17*

Jane confides to Elizabeth how much she likes Bingley, and her surprise that he should ask her to dance twice. Elizabeth exclaims at Jane's modesty and natural goodness; for example, Jane is delighted with Bingley's sisters, while Elizabeth herself is suspicious of them. These sisters have every advantage of money and education and so are condescending, forgetful that their family fortune came from trade. Bingley is a close friend of Darcy, though their characters are totally different. Bingley is easy-going, easily led, well liked. Darcy, though intelligent and sound in judgement, is haughty and offputting, 'continually giving offence' (p. 17).

This chapter successfully develops our view of the main characters. Jane and Bingley are both easily pleased and fall quickly into the classic romantic relationship. Darcy and Elizabeth are more critical, a characteristic that comes from pride in Darcy's case and leads to prejudice in Elizabeth's. Notice how the difference of class and status, so vital to the book, is also carefully established.

Chapter 5, *pp. 18–20*

The Lucases, whose daughter Charlotte is Elizabeth's special friend, visit the Bennets the morning after the ball. Mrs Bennet is upset that Bingley chose Charlotte as his first dancing partner, and reminds the Lucases that he also danced twice with Jane. Darcy's comment about Elizabeth is mentioned and everyone agrees that he is a proud, disagreeable man.

This chapter adds to the climate of near desperation among marriageable women against which the whole book is set. Even dances take on vital significance as signs of affection. Here, too, Darcy's pride and Elizabeth's growing reaction to it, set against a background of general social prejudice, are re-emphasized. You should note too Mary's significant comment defining pride and vanity (p. 20).

Chapter 6, *pp. 21–6*

Jane's friendship with the Bingley sisters develops, but Elizabeth still finds them patronizing. Bingley and Jane become fonder of each other, though Elizabeth is pleased to see that Jane hides her feelings: showing too much would make her vulnerable and open to criticism. Charlotte, however, thinks that a woman should encourage a man's attentions, whether she is attracted to him or not, for fear of losing him. She believes in the practicalities of marriage, for 'happiness . . . is entirely a matter of chance' (p. 22). Elizabeth is horrified at this attitude; only those seeking a rich husband would tolerate an affectionless marriage. She is sure neither she nor Charlotte would stoop so low.

In fact, though unaware of it, Elizabeth is at present attracting a rich husband. Darcy's first unfavourable impressions of her have been replaced by approval of her appearance and 'easy playfulness' (p. 23). At the Lucases' party, he watches her closely and noticing this, Elizabeth teases him, much to Charlotte's embarrassment. Later, chatting to Darcy, Sir William Lucas suggests that Darcy and Elizabeth dance. Uncomfortable lest she appear to be husband-hunting, Elizabeth refuses, and her strong-mindedness attracts Darcy even more. This is noticed by Caroline Bingley who, because she herself hopes to marry Darcy, teases him about his attraction to a member of such an obviously socially inferior family.

In this chapter we see for the first time the idea of marriage as a financial and social contract. It is ironic that eventually both Charlotte and Elizabeth make financially sound marriages, and that Elizabeth's strong condemnation finally turns to understanding and even approval of Charlotte's point of view. Parallel to this, the very rich husband that Elizabeth at first condemns is becoming attracted to her. Notice how Darcy's first impressions of Elizabeth change too, and how much more quickly than her own feelings towards him. She will not encourage him as Charlotte recommends, but simply enjoys baiting him, showing off her wit at his expense. Notice too how Caroline Bingley's jealousy shows itself here, and how Darcy is reminded of the very point which causes problems later in the book: the Bennet family's social inferiority.

Chapter 7, *pp. 27–31*

Mrs Bennet's sister, Mrs Philips, lives in Meryton. At present the younger girls' (Catherine and Lydia) visits to her are motivated by the arrival of a regiment in the town. This is important: it allows for the introduction of Wickham into the book. Notice that right from the start the younger girls' reactions to the soldiers are criticized by their father as being harmful.

No less worrying is that Mrs Bennet encourages Jane to accept an invitation to Netherfield, and to travel there on horseback. She hopes Jane will then have to stay overnight and, thinking that it will help the relationship with Bingley, is delighted when Jane catches a cold and has to remain at Netherfield even longer. Elizabeth walks over to visit her sister and, despite Caroline Bingley's antagonism, she invites Elizabeth to stay and look after Jane.

This incident shows not only Mrs Bennet's matchmaking and Jane's easy agreement to her mother's plans, but also Elizabeth's real concern for Jane. Her walk to Netherfield reveals her impetuosity, and the reactions of Caroline, Bingley and Darcy to her arrival show their characters perfectly.

Chapter 8, *pp. 32–6*

At dinner only Bingley's concern seems to Elizabeth genuinely kind. When she returns to Jane, Caroline criticizes her for walking to Netherfield and jokes again about her 'low connections' (p. 33). On returning downstairs, Elizabeth decides to read rather than play cards: Caroline taunts her for this, turns the talk to Darcy's fine library at Pemberley, and then the conversation moves on to women's accomplishments. Darcy criticizes the contemporary idea that music and needlework alone are sufficient accomplishments and extols the virtues of a mind improved through extensive reading. He knows few accomplished women, he says. To Caroline's annoyance, Elizabeth expresses surprise that he knows any at all.

Although it is a relatively quiet period, the Netherfield visit is important as one of character revelation. It also allows not only Jane and Bingley's romance to develop, but Darcy and Elizabeth to get to know each other. More areas of compatibility appear between them, such as reading. Darcy's definition of the 'accomplished woman' in fact describes Elizabeth exactly. Caroline's jealousy and Bingley's real kindness are also shown in this chapter.

Jane's health now seems worse and it is agreed that a doctor should be sent for in the morning.

Chapter 9, *pp. 37–41*

The doctor calls next morning, as does Mrs Bennet, to see Jane. In an extremely embarrassing scene, she tries to impress Bingley, praising Jane, criticizing Charlotte Lucas and hinting that Bingley should stay on at Netherfield. He replies that his personality makes him act on impulse, and a discussion of characters follows. Elizabeth admits that she enjoys observing all the intricacies and changes of character. Mrs Bennet, totally misunderstanding the conversation, defends social life in the country to everyone's amusement and Elizabeth's shame. The visitors leave, with a final promise from Bingley to Lydia that he will hold a ball.

This chapter brings the Bingleys and Darcy into their closest contact yet with the Bennets, now strengthening Darcy's feelings of superiority which are later to cause so many problems. Elizabeth's comments show her interest in people, but it is ironic that Bingley, whose character she judges as 'estimable' (p. 38), is in fact weak, while the disagreeable Darcy offers, unbeknown to her, a suitably intricate, life-long challenge. Lydia's request to Bingley, which leads to the crucial Netherfield ball, again marks her as being forward and confident, with 'high animal spirits' (p. 40).

Chapter 10, *pp. 42–7*

That evening Caroline Bingley's attraction to Darcy becomes more obvious. She constantly seeks his attention by interrupting him while he writes to Georgiana, which leads eventually to Bingley's intervention. Darcy then criticizes his friend for the impulsiveness he previously admitted to, and for acting too easily on others' suggestions. Elizabeth defends this as being acceptable when the suggestions are offered by friends, while Darcy argues that even a friend should base advice on logic.

Bingley turns the conversation by teasing Darcy about his bad moods and soon after the women are asked to offer musical entertainment. Darcy asks Elizabeth if she wants to dance. She answers him with spirit and is surprised when he answers politely and chivalrously. Darcy's growing feeling for Elizabeth is now obvious to Caroline, who continues to tease him next day in the garden. They meet Elizabeth and Mrs Hurst. The two women join with Darcy, who is embarrassed. Elizabeth, however, is delighted at the opportunity to be on her own.

Darcy and Elizabeth learn more about each other. Her emotion and his logic, later to prove perfect partners, are contrasted in the conversation about Bingley. Notice that both are inconsistent. When Bingley follows a friend's advice (about Jane) Elizabeth is appalled; when Darcy comes to give advice, he gives it illogically.

At this point, with Darcy becoming more and more 'bewitched' (p. 46), Elizabeth is indifferent, and unaware of his feelings. Notice the significance of her delight at being alone at the end of the chapter. In contrast, Caroline Bingley is more attracted by the prospect of marrying Darcy, and even more jealous of Elizabeth.

Chapter 11, *pp. 48–51*

Jane comes downstairs for the first time that evening, and Elizabeth is delighted that Bingley and Jane sit together talking throughout the evening. Caroline, attempting to read a book in order to impress Darcy, cannot gain his interest. She advises Bingley not to have a ball at Netherfield, paces the room to catch his attention and finally, in desperation, asks Elizabeth to walk with her. Then Darcy takes notice, but does not join in because, as he teasingly says, either the ladies wish to talk privately, or they want him to watch them: in either case he will be in the way.

Caroline is offended, and Elizabeth suggests she laugh at Darcy in return. They discuss ridicule. Elizabeth hopes she never laughs at what is 'wise or good' (p. 50) but only at weaknesses. Darcy hopes to avoid such weaknesses; vanity, he says, is such a weakness, but 'pride will be always under good regulation' (p. 51). Elizabeth is amused by his self-ignorance. We learn that Darcy is increasingly afraid of paying her too much attention.

Jane and Bingley's romance is developing well and so, to Caroline's annoyance and his own concern, is Darcy and Elizabeth's. The key conversation here (p. 51) shows both the main characters revealing their pride and prejudice. Elizabeth in fact does ridicule what is both wise and good by mocking Darcy, and is thus guilty of poor judgement based on prejudice. Darcy is confident that his own pride is controlled, and so is Elizabeth.

Both are wrong. Notice, too, the vital distinction made here between vanity and pride.

Chapter 12, *pp. 52–3*

Next morning Elizabeth writes to her mother to arrange for their return home. Although Mrs Bennet wants them to remain as long as possible at Netherfield, it is decided that they should leave the next day. Bingley regrets that they should leave so soon; Caroline regrets that Elizabeth stayed so long and Darcy pointedly ignores Elizabeth for the whole of the last day. When the girls arrive home, the expressions of welcome are mixed – pleasure from Mr Bennet, resentment that they did not stay longer from their mother.

This chapter ends the episode of the Netherfield stay. Notice particularly Darcy's reaction to Elizabeth. Typically proud, he is afraid that he might 'elevate her with the hope of influencing his felicity' (p. 52), therefore he ignores her. Darcy's pride and his misunderstanding of Elizabeth's character, in spite of his supposed love for her, are clearly shown here.

Chapter 13, *pp. 54–7*

Next day, Mr Bennet announces the visit of a stranger, the cousin who will inherit Longbourn when Mr Bennet dies. The stranger's letter requesting the visit shows him to be a clergyman newly appointed to a post at Hunsford under the patronage of one Lady Catherine de Bourgh, mentioned here for the first time. Mrs Bennet is at first outraged by the visit for she will have to entertain the man who will one day take over her estate. She is only softened by hopes of a possible husband for one of her girls. Mr Bennet and Elizabeth guess from the tone of the letter that Mr Collins is somewhat ridiculous, and when he arrives he proves to be just that – a mixture of conceit, servility and exaggerated compliments.

The arrival of the obnoxious Mr Collins begins a new episode in the book, for Collins's courtship of Elizabeth and Charlotte is one of the main events of the following chapters.

Chapter 14, *pp. 58–60*

Collins's first evening at Longbourn is an awkward one. He monopolizes the conversation, talking at length about his patroness Lady Catherine, who seems to be both conceited and officious, but to whom he is embarrassingly grateful. Mr Bennet finds Collins's exaggerated characteristics amusing, but Collins is not so popular with the younger girls. After tea, he reads to them from a book of tedious sermons but Lydia soon interrupts the monotony with her usual chatter about the soldiers. Collins is offended, refuses to read further, and plays backgammon with Mr Bennet instead.

Collins's character is soon well established. He is both ridiculous and conceited, a caricature of pride. Look particularly at the way he refers continually to Lady Catherine to improve his own standing. From this we also gain a clear but negative impression of Lady Catherine before her appearance, so that Wickham's comments in chapter 16 are more believable. Lydia's behaviour continues to be silly and forward.

Chapter 15, *pp. 61–4*

Collins is not 'a sensible man'. His poor upbringing has taught him only the advantages of seeming humble, and the prosperous living has increased his pride. Now, on Lady Catherine's orders, he is to seek a bride. He wishes to marry one of the Bennet girls and so keep Longbourn in the family. He first admires Jane, as the eldest, but on Mrs Bennet's advice turns his attention immediately to Elizabeth. This makes his mercenary nature clear.

Next day, Collins and the girls walk to Meryton. An 'accidental' meeting leads to conversation with one of the army officers and his friend, Wickham, a handsome and charming young man. Darcy and Bingley ride up to talk to the girls, and Elizabeth notices immediately the strained greeting between Darcy and Wickham.

Soon the Bennets move on to their aunt's home, and arrangements are made for an evening party the following day, to which both Collins and Wickham are invited. On the way home, Elizabeth tells Jane about the meeting between Wickham and Darcy, but neither girl can understand what happened.

Here, Collins's character is further developed, as a mixture of 'pride and obsequiousness, self-importance and humility' (p. 61). His practical attitude to marriage is explained, and demonstrated by his instant change of direction from Jane to Elizabeth as a marriage object.

At the same time as Collins's unwelcome proposal becomes more certain, Wickham appears. He is the real romantic interest for Elizabeth. Notice how from the start she is attracted to his appearance which was 'greatly in his favour' (p. 63). Also from the start the confrontation between Wickham and Darcy is made clear, symbolizing what is to follow, their struggle for Elizabeth's belief and trust which continues until Darcy's letter and Elizabeth's change of heart (chs 35–6).

Chapter 16, *pp. 65–72*

Next evening, at the Philipses' party, Wickham immediately joins Elizabeth, who finds him just as interesting and charming as before. Encouraged by learning from her that popular opinion is against Darcy, Wickham condemns him too. Darcy's father, Wickham's benefactor, had intended a church living for him; on his father's death Darcy gave it away, for no other reason, Wickham claims, than their being 'different sort of men, and that he hates me' (p. 68). Elizabeth admits to disliking Darcy, though she had not thought him capable of such wickedness. Nevertheless, a few moments later, she is speaking of Wickham's accusations as proved. Wickham describes his childhood with Darcy, and Darcy's sister, who is also 'very, very proud' (p. 70), and Darcy's capacity for making friends when he wants to. Hearing Collins commenting on Lady Catherine, Wickham then tells Elizabeth that the lady is Darcy's aunt and it is hoped that he and her daughter will marry. Elizabeth is amused, for this means that Caroline Bingley's attentions to Darcy are pointless.

Elizabeth is left with a good impression of Wickham, and much to consider about Darcy. This key conversation provides her with a clear and seemingly logical foundation for her dislike of Darcy which in part leads to her rejection of his proposal. In fact, softened by Wickham's appearance and attentions, she is totally prejudiced for Wickham and against Darcy, and believes everything she is told without rational thought, although she really knows Darcy is not 'so bad as this' (p. 69).

Wickham himself, charming and thoroughly amoral, has enormous self-confidence to lie so blatantly, though he first makes sure he will be believed. Why does he lie? Obviously he wants to protect himself against anything Darcy will say, but there is also a genuine desire to hurt Darcy, whom he hates, and he also wants to impress Elizabeth, whom he is at this time courting. Notice how Elizabeth falls into the trap of a romantic relationship where, as Jane Austen wants us to realize, heart rules head and all sense is lost. She must learn the error of her ways.

We also learn about Darcy's character. Though portrayed through Wickham's biased eyes, we see clearly his wrong pride – and his good pride, which is demonstrated by his family feelings and his charitable actions. Wickham's comments prejudice both Elizabeth and the reader against Darcy, but in fact many of them hint at Darcy's virtues, and so contain an element of truth.

Chapter 17, *pp. 73–5*

Elizabeth tells Jane of Wickham's accusations about Darcy. Jane, true to her character, does not wish to believe ill of either, but Elizabeth 'knows exactly what to think' (p. 73).

The Bingleys arrive with the invitation to the promised ball at Netherfield. The sisters ignore all the family except Jane and leave as soon as possible.

Everyone is excited about the ball, but Elizabeth, who had looked forward to showing her attachment to Wickham by taking the first dances with him, is upset when Collins claims her for them. Mrs Bennet increases her worry by hinting that Collins is about to propose marriage.

The first section of this chapter shows Elizabeth sharing her new view of Darcy with Jane: notice her totally misplaced confidence in her own prejudiced judgement of the situation. Then we are prepared for Collins's proposal, parallel to the development of the relationship Elizabeth would really like to lead to marriage, her friendship with Wickham.

Chapter 18, *pp. 76–87*

The ball at Netherfield is the occasion when Elizabeth hopes to win Wickham's heart. She is therefore both disappointed when the officer does not attend the ball, and angry at Darcy, who she thinks is the cause of Wickham's absence. The dances with Collins are very embarrassing but, to her surprise, Darcy asks her to dance and she unwillingly accepts.

This is Elizabeth's first and only dance with Darcy. In the beginning they talk little, then she teases him about the fact, commenting that both of them dislike small talk, preferring to impress with every word. Next, still angry at Darcy's treatment of Wickham, she mentions him, hinting that she knows the truth: Darcy is embarrassed. They are interrupted by Sir William Lucas, who draws Darcy's attention to Jane and Bingley's obvious romance, and Darcy reacts strangely.

Next, Elizabeth and Darcy discuss books and people's characters. Darcy warns Elizabeth about judging people falsely and too critically, and Elizabeth is angry at what she sees as his denial of his own bad behaviour, though in fact Darcy's criticism of her is correct. They part angrily, but Darcy cannot feel angry with Elizabeth for long.

Elizabeth is now approached by Caroline, who assures her nastily that her attraction to Wickham is misplaced, for he has mistreated Darcy. Convinced that Caroline is prejudiced, Elizabeth ignores her, though Jane confirms the story. Happier discussion of Jane's relationship with Darcy follows, then Mr Collins suggests he introduce himself to Darcy. Elizabeth, realizing that the social difference between them is too great, tries to dissuade him, but Collins approaches Darcy and is snubbed.

The final part of the evening is embarrassing for Elizabeth. Her mother boasts to Lady Lucas of the forthcoming marriage within Darcy's hearing, Mary plays and sings badly, Collins makes a conceited speech putting Darcy down, and the Bennet family overstay their welcome.

Just as Elizabeth has turned against Darcy for his treatment of Wickham, he begins to court her in earnest. Also, unknown to Elizabeth, Darcy is about to end the relationship between Jane and Bingley. Up to this point, he had not realized marriage was a possibility, but having heard Sir William's comments and also seen the Bennets' generally embarrassing behaviour, he becomes concerned.

The chapter shows us Darcy's very real pride and prejudice in his attitude to the Bennets and Collins. In fact, his rejection of Collins is understandable, as Elizabeth herself realizes. Collins, in his presumptuous behaviour, is guilty of more pride than Darcy himself here.

Elizabeth, of course, continues to reject what she sees as prejudiced information from Caroline and even Jane. This is ironic: it is actually she who is prejudiced. Jane's relationship with Bingley is at this stage at its zenith. Notice how Jane Austen does not chart its course in detail. The easy emotion of romantic relationships is of less interest than Elizabeth's and Darcy's hard-won love. Once again, Elizabeth herself is embarrassed by her family's behaviour, paving the way for her acceptance of Darcy's criticism in his letter.

Chapter 19, *pp. 88–92*

The following day Collins begs a private word with Elizabeth; though alarmed, she agrees, if only to get the matter over with.

Collins proposes to her. His proposal reflects his character perfectly. He gives three reasons for marrying: to set an example to his flock, to make himself happy, and to obey his patroness Lady Catherine, who he feels would approve of Elizabeth. Next, Collins explains that he came to Longbourn in search of a wife because he wants the estate to stay in the family. He assures Elizabeth that he will never reproach her for what he knows to be her lack of fortune.

Realizing he is sure she will accept, Elizabeth hurries to thank him and declines the proposal. Collins immediately assumes she is playing courtship games and is undaunted by her refusal, but Elizabeth is sure they would make each other unhappy, and doubts if Lady Catherine would find her suitable. Collins is perturbed at this, but cannot see any reason for her refusal. After all, she cannot afford to be choosy. Elizabeth repeats her answer, and as Collins obviously does not believe her, decides to ask her father to handle the situation.

This is the first of three proposals to Elizabeth in the book. It is obvious that she and Collins are unsuited, that he is an unworthy partner for her. However, he does represent and offer marriage as a financially and socially sound contract which, though she now rejects, Elizabeth comes to see as necessary by the end of the book. Despite this, Collins's proposal is essentially false, in the same way as Darcy's first proposal. It is based on the wrong premises. You should compare it with Darcy's proposal (ch. 34, p. 157), and see why Elizabeth refuses them both and the ways in which she does so.

We learn much of Collins's character in this scene: his pride and stubbornness, his condescension towards Elizabeth. He is also here a comic figure because he is so different from the lover we expect to see. He sees her as the right woman for all the wrong reasons, never truly communicating with her, never understanding her real personality at all. Additionally, we see Elizabeth's strength of character. Though moved to inner laughter, she is courteous and honest, despite the strength of her feelings against Collins. Notice his impression of her as a cunning female. She defends herself as being a 'rational creature' (p. 91) and wants him to see her as such. Can you see anything ironic or amusing in this?

Chapter 20, *pp. 93–6*

Mrs Bennet congratulates Collins on the marriage she assumes will take place, and is alarmed to hear of Elizabeth's refusal. She calls Mr Bennet to order Elizabeth to accept, and with typical good sense he tells Elizabeth not to do so, much to his wife's displeasure. Elizabeth continues to stand firm while her mother pleads and threatens. Finally, Collins withdraws his proposal with apologies and much resentment. Meanwhile, Charlotte arrives to spend the day with the Bennets.

This chapter concludes Collins's proposal by having Mr Bennet support Elizabeth's refusal, thus leaving the way clear for Charlotte's relationship with Collins to develop. Notice here Mrs Bennet's selfish and emotional outburst in front of Elizabeth, in which her concern about the financial side of marriage is much in evidence. We also see Elizabeth's calm, confident handling of emotional pressure, and Collins's petulant reaction to the refusal – only 'his pride was hurt' (p. 95).

Chapter 21, *pp. 97–101*

Apart from Mrs Bennet's distress and Collins's resentment, which is eased by Charlotte Lucas's attention, the problem of the proposal is over. Next day, Elizabeth enjoys meeting Wickham in Meryton, discusses the ball, and when he walks back with her introduces him to her parents. A letter arrives for Jane which obviously upsets her. It is from Caroline. Bingley has, as intended, gone to London, but the others have accompanied him, suggesting he will not return. Whilst in town they hope to see Georgiana, Darcy's sister, whom, Caroline now mentions, it is hoped Bingley will marry. Jane is upset, believing that Caroline is warning her that Bingley's true affections do not lie at Longbourn. Elizabeth argues that Caroline considers her own chances of marrying Darcy will be increased if Bingley weds Georgiana, and so is discouraging Jane deliberately. Jane refuses to think badly of her friend: Elizabeth refuses to believe that Bingley will drop Jane so easily. They both agree not to worry Mrs Bennet with the news.

Notice how subtly Jane Austen here mentions Charlotte's interest in Collins, paving the way for their engagement, and how Elizabeth's hopes are raised by the important step of introducing Wickham to her parents. The two relationships, practical and romantic, run parallel.

The letter is the outward sign of the end of Bingley's first courtship of Jane. This has been ended on Darcy's advice, though we only learn this later. Jane is actually correct in her assessment of the situation and Elizabeth, because of her prejudice for Bingley and against Caroline, is once again misguided.

Chapter 22, *pp. 102–5*

Charlotte Lucas's kindness in distracting Collins after the failed proposal has an ulterior motive – to win him for herself. They meet on Friday morning and the proposal is made and accepted. Charlotte's family is delighted at the news, and she herself, though realizing that Collins is neither 'sensible nor agreeable' (p. 103), has what she wants

– a husband and provision for the future. She remembers, as we should do, her conversation with Elizabeth on the subject of practical marriages and although wary of Elizabeth's feelings she is otherwise happy. Collins, fearing bad reactions, leaves Longbourn on Saturday morning with more overblown thanks, and it is Charlotte who breaks the news to Elizabeth, only to receive an appalled response. Charlotte is sure she will be happy, but Elizabeth, though agreeing for politeness's sake, thinks this is impossible.

Charlotte and Collins's marriage, as we know, is in the nature of a financial and social contract. The motives behind Charlotte's actions are explained in this chapter, as were Collins's in chapter 19, showing the pair to be compatible. Charlotte is practical, clear-sighted, and fully able to handle Collins and their marriage. Elizabeth at this stage thinks such a marriage is 'impossible' (p. 105), but she is wrong and must learn this before forming her own successful relationship with Darcy. Notice how, when Elizabeth tells her of this relationship, Jane at first thinks Elizabeth's marriage to Darcy just as 'impossible' (p. 300) as Elizabeth thinks Charlotte's marriage to Collins to be.

Notice how the quick and easy arrangement of the practical but unromantic marriage contrasts with the protracted course of the relationships of both Jane and Elizabeth.

Chapter 23, *pp. 106–9*

Sir William Lucas arrives at Longbourn with news of the engagement between Charlotte and Collins and is met with total disbelief. Of course, Mrs Bennet is now more upset than ever to think that her best friend's daughter has not only gained a husband but will inherit Longbourn. She is reproachful, the Lucases are triumphant and Elizabeth, disappointed in Charlotte, distances herself from her, particularly as Jane now needs her help. There is no word from London, and even Elizabeth begins to doubt Bingley's faith. Collins returns to Longbourn to arrange the wedding, much to Mrs Bennet's distress.

This is a chapter of reactions, not developments. The Bennets all react predictably to the wedding news, and Elizabeth and Jane react to Bingley's absence. Elizabeth, unwilling to blame Bingley, who seemed so pleasant, blames Darcy and his sisters, thus strengthening her prejudice against Darcy.

Chapter 24, *pp. 113–17*

Caroline writes to confirm that none of her party will return to Nether-field for a while. Jane finally accepts that her relationship with Bingley is over, blaming herself for expecting too much, trying to forget him and to control her emotions. Elizabeth is overwhelmed by Jane's lack of self-interest. She herself is rapidly becoming disillusioned with other people. She condemns Collins, and Charlotte for accepting him, Bingley for his thoughtlessness and Bingley's friends and family for their influence over him. Jane comments that were Bingley fond of her, no influence could part them. Elizabeth disagrees. You might like to compare her reaction to Lady Catherine on the same point later in the book (ch. 56, pp. 286ff.).

Meanwhile, Mrs Bennet is distressed at Bingley's departure. Mr Bennet finds the matter amusing, suggesting that all women benefit from being jilted; Elizabeth should be the next to be jilted, by Wickham. Darcy is hated by everyone in his absence. Social prejudice yet again rears its head.

Here we see the differing characters of Jane and Elizabeth and their views on relationships. Jane is more practical and conventional, accepting that strong emotion is no guarantee of love, yet herself feeling very deeply in the true romantic tradition. Elizabeth is strongly against financially based marriages, believes in the strength of emotions but could, we feel, more easily accept rejection. In fact, Mr Bennet's opinion of relationships, though cynical, has points in its favour. Darcy's possible rejection of Elizabeth after the elopement shows her how much he means to her.

Chapter 25, *pp. 118–21*

At Christmas Collins returns to his parish and Mrs Bennet's brother, Mr Gardiner, arrives at Longbourn with his family. Mrs Gardiner is a special friend of Elizabeth. Their first conversation concerns Jane. Mrs Gardiner is sceptical of Elizabeth's opinion that Bingley seemed genuinely involved. She says that young men fall in and out of love easily. She suggests a visit to London to distract Jane who, unlike Elizabeth, cannot make light of her sadness. Mrs Gardiner in fact watches Elizabeth closely and is worried by her obvious attachment to Wickham, who visits Longbourn a great deal over Christmas.

Mrs Gardiner is introduced in this chapter. She is an 'amiable, intelligent, elegant' woman (p. 118) and we feel that had she been Elizabeth's mother life would have been very different for the heroine. Mrs Gardiner's real concern for the girls, and the practical comments she makes, are the first mature help Elizabeth has received and accepted. Through it she begins to see violent emotion in relationships as something to be examined rationally, not to be taken on face value. Is Mrs Gardiner right about Bingley's affection and its effect on Jane?

Chapter 26, *pp. 122–6*

In their second conversation, Mrs Gardiner tactfully advises Elizabeth not to encourage Wickham, for as neither has any fortune the relationship would be impossible. Elizabeth at first argues, blames Darcy for Wickham's situation, and points out that young people often marry without money. In the end she knows Mrs Gardiner to be right and resolves to 'do my best' (p. 123).

Charlotte and Collins marry and return to Hunsford. Charlotte writes often, seems happy with everything and eager to renew the friendship with Elizabeth who, despite her misgivings, agrees to visit them in March. Jane returns to London with the Gardiners. Hearing nothing from Caroline she visits her and receives a polite but cold welcome; the return visit is equally as brief and resentful. Jane realizes that her relationship with Bingley is at an end, particularly as Caroline has hinted that he knows Jane is in London and yet has not attempted to see her.

Meanwhile, Wickham has turned his attentions to Mary King, a new heiress. Elizabeth writes to tell Mrs Gardiner that she cannot after all have been in love with him because she feels little pain at the news.

Three relationships change in parallel in this chapter. Charlotte and Collins mark the success of theirs by marriage; Jane abandons all hope of Bingley; Wickham jilts Elizabeth.

The theme of marriage for money is highlighted by Mrs Gardiner's advice and Wickham's courtship of an heiress. Elizabeth at first wants to ignore financial matters: 'where there is affection, young people are seldom withheld by . . . want of fortune' (p. 122). It would, however, have been an impoverished, unworkable match and she knows it. She allows affection to blind her to the practical realities of the situation, defending Wickham both in his courtship of her and in his subsequent attentions to Mary King. Later when she realizes her prejudice, both his actions seem totally 'mercenary' (p. 170).

Notice also in this chapter Caroline's propensity for vicious lying, Mrs Gardiner's tactful good sense and Jane's passive benevolence.

Chapter 27, *pp. 127-9*

In March Elizabeth goes to Hunsford with Sir William and Maria Lucas. She is by now looking forward to the visit, her only regret being that she must leave her father. Wickham and she part as friends, he remembering that she was the first to attract him, she considering that he will always be 'her model of the amiable and pleasing' (p. 127).

The party stops at London. Jane seems composed, but Elizabeth learns from Mrs Gardiner that she is often depressed. Mrs Gardiner next criticizes Wickham, pointing out that he paid Mary King no attention at all until she came into her fortune. Elizabeth defends him: why is it wrong to marry both without a fortune and for the sake of it? Mrs Gardiner warns her against bitterness and then, to Elizabeth's delight, invites her on a tour of the Lakes that summer, an invitation which is later to prove vital to the plot.

This chapter marks the transition between episodes: the end of Elizabeth's first period at Longbourn, the start of her visit to Hunsford. It is also the end of her innocent, uncritical opinion of Wickham. Affection for him bids her defend Wickham and she criticizes Darcy and Bingley; but by the time she returns to Longbourn, her views will be reversed. It is at this point that Elizabeth's childhood ends.

Chapter 28, *pp. 130–33*

Elizabeth and the Lucases arrive at Hunsford. Charlotte greets them affectionately, Collins with his usual ostentation. He wants Elizabeth to see what she has missed. The house is pleasant, Charlotte seems happy, though it is only by ignoring Collins that she achieves content-ment. At dinner, Collins mentions Lady Catherine, and suggests they might expect an invitation to dinner. Next day Lady Anne stops at the vicarage with just such an invitation. Elizabeth is pleased to see that she is 'sickly and cross', the perfect wife for Darcy (p. 133).

This chapter begins the stay at Hunsford and time spent at Rosings. It becomes clear to Elizabeth that, though it is loveless, Charlotte's marriage works: 'it was all done very well' (p. 132). We see here that Elizabeth's judgements can be wrong, and that practical marriages do have their place. Jane Austen also begins to prepare us for Elizabeth's meetings with Lady Catherine, through Collins's references, and Lady Anne's visit.

Chapter 29, *pp. 134–9*

Despite Collins's fussing, Elizabeth remains calm and confident during her visit to Rosings. The house and grounds are impressive, Lady Catherine formidable, Lady Anne insignificant. After dinner, in the drawing-room, the ladies listen to their hostess's opinions, instructions and advice. She questions Elizabeth impertinently about her accomplishments, education and age, but Elizabeth answers her confidently. We learn that the Bennet girls had a free education without the benefit of a governess, and are all 'out', the younger attending balls before the older ones are married. The evening ends with cards and the drive home is taken up with Collins continuing to praise his patroness.

We here meet Lady Catherine, a comic character and an example of one whose false pride delights in using its power to manipulate others. We also learn about Elizabeth's girlhood, and her development as one whom Darcy would call truly accomplished. You might like to consider the freedom the Bennets have given their children. Have they benefited from it? Are the Bennets good parents?

Chapter 30, *pp. 140–42*

After a week, Sir William returns to Meryton and Elizabeth settles down to life at Hunsford; this takes the form of long walks, conversations with Charlotte and visits to Rosings. During this time she realizes how well Charlotte is making her marriage work.

A fortnight later, just before Easter, Darcy visits his aunt with a cousin, one Colonel Fitzwilliam. When Collins pays his respects, the gentlemen return to the Parsonage with him to visit Elizabeth. Colonel Fitzwilliam proves to be a true gentleman, and Elizabeth is immediately attracted to him, but Darcy is his usual haughty self. Elizabeth provokes him by asking whether he has seen Jane while in London. He seems embarrassed. Soon after, the gentlemen leave.

Whilst appreciating even more the value of the practical marriage, Elizabeth meets Darcy again, and so begins that train of events which will lead to his proposal. Colonel Fitzwilliam is also introduced, providing another admirer for Elizabeth. Notice the irony of Elizabeth's comment to Darcy about Jane. At this point, she does not realize he is responsible for Bingley's ending the relationship.

Chapter 31, *pp. 143–6*

On the next visit to Rosings Colonel Fitzwilliam, who has taken a
liking to Elizabeth, talks to her eagerly. Darcy watches them curiously
(what might he be feeling?) and Lady Catherine, feeling excluded,
interrupts the conversation to criticize Elizabeth's lack of musical
accomplishment. Colonel Fitzwilliam persuades Elizabeth to play and
Darcy moves closer to look at her. She meets his stare and accuses him
of being aloof and anti-social. Darcy claims he is uncomfortable in
unfamiliar company, but Elizabeth retorts that he merely lacks practice,
as she does on the piano. Darcy now compliments Elizabeth as a truly
accomplished woman, adding 'we neither of us perform to strangers'
(p. 146), meaning that both of them reveal their true selves only to
those closest to them. The conversation is ended once more by Lady
Catherine's interruption.

   Here, Darcy comes very close to revealing how much he admires
Elizabeth, hinting that they might, as a partnership, open their hearts
to each other. Do you think Elizabeth understands what Darcy is
saying? Does he think she does? Notice also Colonel Fitzwilliam's
developing attraction towards Elizabeth and Lady Catherine's jealousy.

Chapter 32, *pp. 147–50*

Next morning Darcy visits the Parsonage and finds Elizabeth alone.
She straightaway mentions the sudden departure of the Netherfield
party the previous November but, for reasons we know, Darcy will
only comment that Bingley will probably cease renting Netherfield.
The talk turns to the Collinses, the success of their marriage, the
distance of family homes from marital ones. Darcy tests Elizabeth's
reaction to the thought of moving from Longbourn. He withdraws a
little when she shows surprise and the conversation ends with the
return of Charlotte and Maria. When Charlotte suggests Darcy is 'in
love with you' (p. 149), Elizabeth laughs.

   Darcy and Colonel Fitzwilliam now visit the Parsonage almost every day. Elizabeth admires the Colonel, for he reminds her of Wickham, but Darcy always seems silent and withdrawn.

This chapter continues to set the scene for the proposal: Darcy is in love and ready to take Elizabeth back to Pemberley with him, feeling she is too good for Longbourn. How much does Elizabeth understand his feelings or her own? Notice how Elizabeth here makes a public statement of her approval of the Collinses' practical marriage, and how it is the clear-sighted Charlotte who suspects the truth of the romantic situation which is developing.

Chapter 33, *pp. 151–5*

Elizabeth regularly walks in the park and Darcy often meets her, continuing his undeclared courtship. One day, Colonel Fitzwilliam joins her, and after Elizabeth has criticized both him and Darcy for their riches and power, the conversation turns to marriage. Younger sons, says the Colonel, cannot marry where they wish, but must consider fortune. Embarrassed at the suggestion that she is too poor for him, Elizabeth changes the subject and mentions Darcy's sister, asking whether she is as 'difficult to manage' (p. 152) as Darcy. Colonel Fitzwilliam looks at Elizabeth sharply, but she reassures him that she knows nothing bad about Georgiana.

The Colonel believes Darcy recently saved Bingley from an imprudent marriage: there were 'very strong objections' (p. 153) against the lady. Elizabeth is horrified, can only comment that Darcy had no right to interfere, then avoids the subject until they reach the Parsonage. Once alone she breaks down, realizing that it was not a natural change in Bingley's affection that caused Jane's suffering, but Darcy's interference. Why should he have interfered? Elizabeth can only think of her family's trade connections and her mother's tactlessness, and decides that it is really Darcy's pride and his wish that Bingley marry Georgiana that are to blame. She feels so unwell that she cannot go to Rosings that evening.

This chapter is the first of three which herald the turning point of the book. Elizabeth has yet another condemnation of Darcy to fuel her prejudice. Believing him to be totally motivated by pride, she lets her biased emotions rule her head, without reasoning through the possible alternatives or the rational arguments in Darcy's favour. However, do consider that she is motivated by concern for those she loves and that on the face of it Darcy's actions are interfering and wrong. Notice too how, having reminded Elizabeth of the importance of fortune in marriage and having played his part in telling her of Darcy's actions, Colonel Fitzwilliam does not appear again in the book.

Chapter 34, *pp. 156–60*

Reading Jane's letters that evening, Elizabeth is interrupted by Darcy. To Elizabeth's complete astonishment he suddenly confesses his love for her. At first flattered, though not tempted to accept him, she soon realizes that Darcy speaks out of 'pride' as well as 'tenderness' (p. 157). Assuming Elizabeth will accept, he is intent on letting her know how much he is lowering himself by marrying her. Insulted, Elizabeth retorts that she cannot return his feelings or feel grateful. She does not want his love and even now he seems to begrudge giving it.

Darcy is surprised and resentful. Elizabeth adds that she cannot forgive his treatment of Wickham and Jane. Darcy argues that he acted for the best and only wishes he could have curbed his own romantic feelings too.

Darcy now turns on Elizabeth. It is really her pride that is wounded. Had he wooed and flattered her, she would have accepted. Elizabeth flings the accusation of pride in his face: Darcy should have behaved in a more 'gentleman-like manner' (p. 159). As it is, she could never marry him.

Darcy leaves angrily. Elizabeth is left to wonder at what has happened. Though secretly flattered that Darcy could love her, his pride and callousness only anger her. Here Darcy clearly reveals his pride, his class prejudice, forthrightness, and his lack of a genuine love; if Darcy really did love Elizabeth, her inferior social standing would be of no importance. Affected by this Elizabeth reacts just as strongly. She is flattered and grateful, but she points out to Darcy the falseness of his feelings. Of course, she is also prejudiced and influenced by her feelings for Jane and Wickham. But her pride is hurt.

The proposal is a turning point for both. Elizabeth's accusation that Darcy is ungentlemanly stops him emotionally in his tracks; it 'tortured' (p. 296) him, as he later admits. As never before, someone he admires has criticized his pride. A true hero, he learns from this: he storms out 'ashamed' (p. 160) of his love, but from then on he honestly tries to overcome his pride and to love Elizabeth fully. Elizabeth too learns more about herself. Though she does not yet admit it, Darcy's point about vanity strikes home. She also realizes that he loves her, and this is the beginning of a long process whereby she learns to return that love.

The chapter certainly shows the negative aspects of relationships. Darcy's infatuation is false and Elizabeth rightly rejects it. But Elizabeth's preference for romantic love is equally wrong. Both are misguided in their view of the financial and social considerations of marriage. Yet, even when quarrelling, both characters show they can form the basis of a good relationship. They communicate; they listen and afterwards act on what they hear; they move towards a desire for the other's good and a growth in themselves.

Compare this proposal with Collins's proposal in chapter 16, looking at the characters, the way they communicate with and regard each other, and the ultimate outcome of each proposal.

Chapter 35, *pp. 161–7*

Next morning, while walking in the park, Elizabeth meets Darcy who hands her a letter. It explains first that he realized at the Netherfield ball that Jane and Bingley's relationship seemed certain to lead to marriage. However, he felt Jane's feelings were shallow. He was also conscious of the Bennets' poor connections and, worse, the lack of propriety shown by all except Elizabeth and Jane. So with Caroline Bingley's help, Darcy convinced Bingley of Jane's indifference and persuaded him to end the relationship.

Darcy also reveals Wickham as a weak and dissolute character. Darcy was content when he said that he preferred to enter the Law rather than the Church, and he gave him good compensation for the lost living. Later, Wickham changed his mind, and when Darcy refused to grant him the post, revenged himself by planning an elopement with Georgiana. This was prevented only at the last moment when Georgiana confided in Darcy. To avoid family scandal, Darcy kept this secret. The letter concludes with the suggestion that Elizabeth should verify the story with Colonel Fitzwilliam.

This is the first time that Darcy himself expresses his views and feelings. His statement is still proud and defensive, and intent on not 'humbling myself' (p. 162), but at least he does give an explanation.

The letter is logical, well-argued and reasonable – all the virtues Darcy's character possesses and Elizabeth's judgement lacks. It reveals the stories developed in chapters 16 and 33 in a totally different light, showing Elizabeth and the reader just how easy it is to be taken in.

What does it show of Darcy's character? His decision about Bingley's relationship with Jane is proud and overbearing, based on an incorrect opinion of Jane and a prejudiced view of her family. However, he is clear-sighted enough to see romance realistically, and to protect his friend from his own weakness. As far as Wickham is concerned Darcy's behaviour seems blameless, Georgiana's confidence in him shows the trustworthiness of his character, and we must also realize that in telling Elizabeth of the elopement, Darcy risks her using the information in anger against him.

This letter and its statement of Darcy's position leads to Elizabeth's change of heart in the next chapter.

Chapter 36, *pp. 168–72*

Elizabeth reads Darcy's letter 'with a strong prejudice' (p. 168), not believing his account of the Jane and Bingley episode. Over the story of Wickham, though, she is less certain. Putting the letter away, she walks on, but almost immediately rereads it, showing her willingness to face the truth.

Elizabeth realizes she knows very little about Wickham; she accepts his charm without question, but can think of nothing positively good that he has actually done. Darcy's story of the planned elopement is supported by Colonel Fitzwilliam's reaction to her comment about Georgiana. Elizabeth then questions Wickham's confiding in her at all, his making the story public and not attending the ball. His attentions to Mary King and to herself suddenly seem 'mercenary' (p. 170). Conversely Darcy, though proud, has never acted wrongly; he is valued by those who know him, and is affectionate towards his sister and friends.

Elizabeth realizes (pp. 170–71) that she had been blind and prejudiced, that her respective judgements of Wickham and Darcy have been totally wrong, based on vanity influenced by their attitudes towards her, and that up to now 'I never knew myself' (p. 171). This is the heart of the chapter and in many ways the heart of the novel. From now on, Elizabeth's eyes are opened and she begins to mature.

The first sign of her increasing maturity is that on rereading the account of Jane and Bingley's relationship, Elizabeth realizes the truth of Darcy's comments: Jane *does* seem indifferent to Bingley, the family *is* inferior.

Worn out by so much thought, Elizabeth returns to the Parsonage. Darcy and Colonel Fitzwilliam have already made their farewells and left.

This chapter marks the key change in Elizabeth. From now on she tries to see things clearly. In fact, by the end of the chapter, she has actually reasoned matters through rationally and emotionally. She now knows the true natures of both Wickham and Darcy, the real reason for Bingley's departure, the truth about her family, and her own faults of pride and prejudice. She does not yet care enough for Darcy, but she has begun to respect and value him. From this point on, she sets aside thoughts of Wickham, Colonel Fitzwilliam and romantic love and turns her attention to the reality of Darcy.

Chapter 37, *pp. 173–6*

Darcy and Colonel Fitzwilliam leave Rosings the next morning and the presence of the Hunsford party is again requested at Rosings. Lady Catherine notices that Elizabeth is not herself and high-handedly suggests that she stay longer at the Parsonage, condescending to offer a servant and carriage for the journey home. This episode not only brings Elizabeth and the reader down to earth, but also allows Elizabeth to consider what would happen if she were to accept a proposal from Darcy and thus become related to Lady Catherine.

Elizabeth considers the letter, feeling both regret and gratitude, but has no wish to see Darcy ever again. She is particularly upset by his comments about her family and realizes that Lydia and Kitty are especially silly and weak. What event is Jane Austen preparing us for here?

Depressed by thoughts of Jane and Wickham, Elizabeth passes the final week at Hunsford.

Chapter 38, *pp. 177–9*

Elizabeth leaves Hunsford. Her thanks to Collins for the visit are sincere, though she cannot join in his praise of Lady Catherine. Collins also states that his marriage is happy because he and Charlotte are so similar (you might like to ask yourself whether this is true), and Elizabeth honestly agrees that it is a good match. The party leave for London where they stay before returning to Longbourn with Jane.

This transitional chapter takes us from Hunsford to London.

Elizabeth here makes her final judgement on Charlotte's marriage: although she does not regret refusing Collins, she realizes the error of her original reasons for the rejection.

Chapter 39, *pp. 180–83*

The next section of the book, the time between Elizabeth's visits to Hunsford and Derbyshire, begins with the journey from London. Kitty and Lydia meet the party on the way. Lydia had promised to treat the girls to dinner, but has spent her money on a bonnet she herself admits is ugly. She gossips about men and dances, and confesses that she would like to marry before her older sisters. She reveals that Wickham is now free, for Mary King has gone to Liverpool.

Once home again everyone is glad to see them. Lydia busily tells everyone about their journey and says she hopes to go to Brighton, as the regiment is moving there. For the first time we hear Lydia talk at length and see her as a real character; she is immature, self-centred, impractical, interested only in flirtation and marriage. Why should Jane Austen concentrate on Lydia now? What relevance has Wickham's freedom to this?

Chapter 40, *pp. 184–7*

Elizabeth soon tells Jane about Darcy's proposal. Shocked, Jane really wants to believe that both Darcy and Wickham had behaved correctly. She comments on Wickham's apparent goodness, and Elizabeth replies that he may appear good, but it is in fact Darcy who is the worthier. She regrets disliking and mocking Darcy, and is beginning to realize that in spite of her contrary belief, she does make the mistake of laughing at what is 'wise or good' (p. 50). The sisters decide not to reveal Wickham's true nature, and Elizabeth also conceals from Jane Darcy's part in Bingley's absence. Mrs Bennet mentions Jane's unhappiness and also inquires resentfully after Charlotte and Collins.

Elizabeth shows here that she does not hide her faults – she admits them to Jane and is already trying to change. Notice, though, the decision not to reveal Wickham's character. It contributes to Lydia's elopement, as Elizabeth herself later realizes. Is it totally motivated by kindness or is Elizabeth unwilling to admit she has been deceived?

Chapter 41, *pp. 188–93*

The regiment is leaving Meryton. Mrs Bennet and the younger girls are heartbroken, but Elizabeth, remembering Darcy's comments, is ashamed for them.

Lydia, however, is invited to accompany the regiment to Brighton. Elizabeth is sincerely afraid that her sister will make a fool of herself. She warns her father, but he thinks Lydia needs to go in order to learn the realities of life and her own insignificance. He rebukes Elizabeth for worrying that Lydia's behaviour will reflect badly on her and Jane.

Elizabeth now sees Wickham for the last time. She is annoyed because he is trying to court her again now that Mary King has gone. She hints broadly that she knows the truth about Darcy and him and now appreciates Darcy's true character. Wickham is embarrassed. The regiment leaves, and Lydia goes too.

In this chapter, we see more of Lydia's self-centred, flighty character; her visit to Brighton begins, giving her the opportunity, away from her family, to elope with Wickham. The beginning of her relationship with him is paralleled by the end of his relationship with Elizabeth, who now sees the difference between 'appearance' (p. 192) and reality. The other important scene is between Elizabeth and Mr Bennet, who shows a paternal weakness by allowing Lydia to go to Brighton. Is he right in saying that anyone who truly values Jane or Elizabeth will not be put off by the rest of the family?

Chapter 42, *pp. 194–8*

The Bennets' marriage is an unhappy one. Now that the personal attraction has faded, Mr Bennet has no respect for his wife, and he delights in mocking her. Because of Darcy's comments, Elizabeth is especially aware at this time of the disadvantages of her family background.

With the regiment gone, life is dull. Lydia's letters are uninformative. Elizabeth looks forward to her holiday in the Lakes but the plans have to be changed. The holiday is cut short and the party decide to go only to Derbyshire. They arrive at Lambton, not far from Pemberley, and Mrs Gardiner suggests visiting the house. Once Elizabeth is told that the family is not there, she agrees.

This chapter begins by describing the failure of a marriage made from affection and physical attraction and its bad effects on the offspring. It also marks the end of Elizabeth's stay at Longbourn and the start of her second holiday. Notice how Elizabeth's periods away from home are eventful and productive. She is busier and she also matures. Why should this be?

Chapter 43, *pp. 201–11*

To Elizabeth, Pemberley and its grounds are a perfect combination of natural and man-made beauty. For the first time, she realizes that 'to be mistress of Pemberley might be something' (p. 201).

The party looks at some miniatures, first of Wickham, who the housekeeper says has turned out 'wild', and then Darcy, who she declares is sweet-natured and good to both his sister and to the poor. Elizabeth is amazed, having always considered Darcy to be bad-tempered. Upstairs she sees a portrait of Darcy and finds to her surprise that the portrait and housekeeper's comments about him together make her like him more than ever before.

The party next walks outside. Suddenly, Darcy appears. Both he and Elizabeth are embarrassed, but he greets her politely and gently before taking his leave. Elizabeth is struck by the change in him. This is the first hint we have that Darcy has also had a change of heart.

Later, Darcy meets them again. Elizabeth introduces the Gardiners and is pleased that he seems impressed by them. He mentions that the Bingleys are to visit, with Georgiana, whom he would like Elizabeth to meet; this is a real sign of respect.

Driving back to Lambton, the Gardiners seem amazed at Darcy's kindness, and Elizabeth has to hint that her original judgement of him was mistaken, just as it was of Wickham.

The first section of this chapter, where Elizabeth sees how Darcy lives, shows her that he has taste, elegance, a talent for combining the best of nature and the man-made, and that he can be kind and good-tempered. Darcy has already admitted he does not open his heart to strangers (ch. 31). It is only at Pemberley that Elizabeth sees the real Darcy. Now the next stage in the proceedings begins: their first meeting following their respective changes of heart. This shows Elizabeth that Darcy has changed and, in addition, she is now seeing him without prejudice. She not only sees him as someone for whom she could feel respect and gratitude, but also as someone likeable. For his part, he has lost much of his pride and is now considering Elizabeth's feelings as he properly should. His meeting the Gardiners, Elizabeth's 'real' parents, shows him that her 'family' does include noteworthy people.

Chapter 44, *pp. 212–17*

Darcy brings Georgiana to see Elizabeth on the day she arrives, a great compliment. Bingley also appears. Elizabeth is pleased to find he seems unattracted to Georgiana, but inquires after Jane. Darcy is as desirous as ever to please. Mr and Mrs Gardiner see in fact that he 'knew what it was to love' (p. 213) and they approve of him.

Elizabeth reconsiders her feelings. She now wants to please Darcy, and has a 'real interest in his welfare' (p. 216). She wonders whether to encourage a second proposal.

Meeting Georgiana is important. It proves Darcy's real trust in Elizabeth. Bingley appears again, marking the renewal of his romantic relationship with Jane, though they do not yet meet. Darcy's love is now judged by the Gardiners to be genuine; we trust their judgement and Elizabeth begins to think of marriage as a real possibility.

Chapter 45, *pp. 218–21*

Next day the party visit Pemberley again and meet the Bingley sisters. It is obvious that Caroline still wants to marry Darcy. She sarcastically comments to Elizabeth that the regiment's departure must be a 'great loss to your family' (p. 219). Caroline is baiting Elizabeth with references to Wickham, but though this scarcely touches Elizabeth, it embarrasses Georgiana. Elizabeth reacts well though, Georgiana recovers, and Darcy thinks even more highly of Elizabeth. When the party leave, Caroline criticizes Elizabeth's looks, manner and 'self-sufficiency' (p. 221). Darcy is annoyed and defends her.

Here, Elizabeth shows her indifference to Wickham and her calmness in the face of this attack helps Georgiana, strengthening her bond with Darcy. Also, Caroline, her rival, is at last defeated by Elizabeth's behaviour and Darcy's reactions. We feel confident now of a second proposal and are lulled into a false sense of security before the expected elopement.

Chapter 46, *pp. 222–8*

Elizabeth receives two letters from Jane. One says that Lydia has eloped to Scotland with Wickham. Jane, of course, believes it is for the best, and that Wickham intends to marry Lydia. The second letter reveals that Wickham did not intend to go to Gretna Green, or in fact to marry at all. Colonel Forster has traced the couple as far as London and he and Mr Bennet are now trying to find them there.

Elizabeth is horrified by this news. Darcy arrives, and she is so concerned that she discloses the contents of the letters to him. Elizabeth blames herself for not revealing Wickham's true character; Darcy becomes silent and thoughtful and soon takes his leave. Elizabeth is convinced that this proof of her family's impropriety has killed his love, and is upset. She realizes that though Lydia probably believed that Wickham intended to marry her, in fact her original attraction to him could only have been physical. The Gardiners arrive and are very concerned. Almost immediately, they set off for London.

Lydia's elopement is revealed in this chapter. It is representative of relationships based on sexual attraction and as such is condemned by Jane Austen through Elizabeth. We realize that Wickham is in fact far more vicious than we ever thought for, as Elizabeth sees, he has no intention of marrying. Lydia is not so much morally wrong as socially irresponsible and horribly innocent. She is also now in real danger. A ruined woman is unmarriageable and very vulnerable, so Elizabeth's reaction is not as exaggerated as it might seem. Consider, though, one critical comment that Elizabeth's judgement of Lydia is in fact harsher than that of Wickham. Why should this be?

For Elizabeth, the news changes everything. Her family is obviously truly inferior to Darcy's. Fearing that he will cease to love her, she realizes how much he means to her, and from now on she actively seeks his love.

In fact, unbeknown to Elizabeth, Darcy does not condemn her. His family had once been similarly threatened. He has overcome his pride and prejudice, and he has left only in order to do what he can to help. Notice that this is the first time Elizabeth has actually shown that she needs help. Her needs are met more fully than she could have hoped.

Chapter 47, *pp. 229–37*

This and the following chapters follow the discovery of Lydia and Wickham in London and the arrangement of their marriage. The events are revealed mainly through a series of letters, a method of story-telling used in many of the novels of the time.

During the journey back to Longbourn, Elizabeth and the Gardiners speculate on whether Wickham will marry Lydia. Elizabeth comments on her sister's character and how her upbringing has damaged her. She also tells the Gardiners what she knows about Wickham's true character. Like Darcy, she blames herself for what has happened. Back at Longbourn, Jane and Elizabeth comfort each other and, with their mother, Elizabeth reads Lydia's parting letter.

For Elizabeth, as for the reader, this is a time of suspended action, uncertainty and worry. We learn that she regrets concealing Wickham's real nature, and her view of her sister as 'thoughtless' (p. 236) is compounded. Lydia has no idea of the effect of her action on the family or herself.

Chapter 48, *pp. 238–42*

Mr Gardiner sets off next morning for London. His first letter tells how he has met Mr Bennet, but has no news. The next letter to arrive is from Collins. It contains only pompous condolences and a quite unchristian condemnation of Lydia. Mr Gardiner's next letter still has little news except that Wickham has incurred heavy gambling debts. Mr Bennet has been persuaded to return home. He arrives the following day, as calm and philosophical as usual. He does, however, remind Elizabeth that she had warned him not to let Lydia visit Brighton and that he had ignored her advice.

There is little action in this chapter. Collins's letter reveals his hypocrisy and lack of charity and Mr Bennet shows his likeable character in his admission to Elizabeth. The chapter also marks the passage of time since the elopement.

Chapter 49, *pp. 243–8*

Two days later, Mr Gardiner writes again. The couple have been found. Although Wickham had no intention of marrying Lydia, he has agreed to do so for a small financial settlement.

Mr Bennet realizes at once that Wickham has been given money to marry. Believing it is Mr Gardiner's doing, he wonders how to repay him. Elizabeth, meanwhile, though glad that Lydia's future is secure, seriously questions the idea of such an unsuitable marriage: 'And for *this* we are to be thankful?' (p. 245). The girls tell Mrs Bennet, who immediately forgets the horror of the past weeks and rejoices at the thought of a married daughter at last.

The marriage is arranged, but the problems are obvious. Lack of true affection is paralleled by lack of money, and, in effect, Wickham has been bribed to marry Lydia. Elizabeth shows her independence and sensitivity when she questions a society that prefers a loveless marriage for the sake of reputation to no marriage at all. Mrs Bennet's reactions to the marriage are very wrong, showing no real awareness of the moral problems of Wickham's true character. Interested only in the status of marriage, she ignores the truth about this one.

Chapter 50, *pp. 249–53*

When the Bennets married, they had at first been confident that they would bear a son to inherit their estate. By the time their five daughters had been born it was too late to start saving; now there will be no income after Mr Bennet's death. He is therefore grateful that Lydia will be provided for at so little cost.

Elizabeth meanwhile regrets that she ever told Darcy about the elopement, for there now seems no need for anyone to learn what has happened. She knows that Darcy cannot be expected to marry into a disgraced family, particularly now that Wickham, his enemy, is a part of it. She realizes too that Darcy and she are in fact perfectly suited. He would have 'answered all her wishes' (p. 252), but, it seems, the marriage will now never happen.

News of the wedding spreads. Mr Bennet refuses Lydia money for clothes but eventually allows the couple to visit Longbourn after the wedding. Afterwards Wickham is to join a northern regiment.

This chapter continues to show the importance of the financial side of marriage. Like Lydia and Wickham's, the Bennets' relationship had been based on physical attraction; it is an unhappy and financially unstable marriage. Against the background of these two failing relationships, Elizabeth now sees clearly that Darcy is the answer to her wishes. Her belief that marriage to him is now impossible makes her realize how much she values him.

This is a key scene in Elizabeth's development, marking the point where she learns that the right relationship is the one that meets, answers, complements – not the one that flatters and agrees.

Chapter 51, *pp. 254–8*

Lydia is married and afterwards visits Longbourn with Wickham for ten days. Only Mrs Bennet greets them without distress, but the couple seem unembarrassed. Wickham is as charming as ever but, as Elizabeth expects, does not return Lydia's affection equally. Lydia is still wild, chattering on about her elopement, her ring and her married status. She describes her wedding to Elizabeth and Jane, letting slip the fact that Darcy had attended. Elizabeth is amazed and rather than question Lydia, writes for news to Mrs Gardiner.

We now see the results of Lydia and Wickham's marriage. Lydia's irresponsible, self-centred nature is shown in detail. Wickham's appearance is unchanged, though we now know all about him. Neither Lydia nor Wickham has changed because of their love. Compare Elizabeth and Darcy, whose growing relationship has greatly improved both their characters. The other main event of this chapter is Elizabeth's discovery that Darcy was at the wedding. It reveals to her his true generosity.

Chapter 52, *pp. 259–65*

Mrs Gardiner replies to Elizabeth's letter, expressing surprise that she had not been aware of the build-up to recent events. Darcy, feeling responsible for the elopement, had tracked the couple down. Lydia claimed she did not need help, since she was sure they would be married. Wickham blamed Lydia for accompanying him to London and said that he intended to make a rich match elsewhere. Darcy bribed him with money and a commission to make him marry Lydia, and he persuaded Mr Gardiner, despite his reluctance, to let him pay. Lydia, while staying with the Gardiners, seemed ungrateful and unaware of what she had done. Mrs Gardiner ends her letter by hinting that it would be a good thing if Elizabeth were to marry Darcy.

Elizabeth is overcome by all that Darcy has done and, whilst hoping it is because of her, she cannot allow herself to expect so.

Wickham interrupts Elizabeth while she is reading the letter. She mentions Darcy's housekeeper's comments about Wickham, and he then has the effrontery to mention meeting Darcy in London, thinking Elizabeth does not know the reason for the meeting. She in turn baits him by referring to Anne de Bourgh and Georgiana. Elizabeth then charges Wickham that his original tale to her was inaccurate, showing clearly that she knows the truth. Wickham is embarrassed, but does not admit he lied. Elizabeth suggests they forget the past, and they part amicably.

Now Elizabeth learns the extent to which Darcy has helped Lydia and, though she dares not admit it, herself. Darcy is shown as a truly good character who has overcome his prejudice and pride to do right. Her feelings towards him are even more positive and she now has the clear approval of Mrs Gardiner, whose advice she values, for marriage with Darcy. Elizabeth tells Wickham she knows the truth, showing us that she can no longer be taken in and is safe from charm such as his. We should not expect Wickham to admit he lied here – it would be out of character – but he is at least embarrassed. Notice finally too how Lydia remains insensitive and ungrateful to the end, even to Mrs Gardiner.

Chapter 53, *pp. 266–72*

Lydia and Wickham leave for Newcastle: Mrs Bennet is depressed but rallies when she hears Bingley is returning to Netherfield. Jane refuses to admit that this news affects her, but Elizabeth hopes for the best.

Bingley visits Netherfield with Darcy, and Elizabeth is both embarrassed and unsure of his feelings. Bingley is received warmly but Mrs Bennet, still believing that Darcy treated Wickham badly, embarrassingly snubs him. Darcy himself seems uncomfortable, and this depresses Elizabeth.

But all true love must be tested, and Elizabeth, who is given hope by Darcy's arrival, must doubt that he still cares before she can fully realize what she feels. Darcy is now seen to reassess Jane and Bingley's relationship and also Elizabeth's feelings. Remember that he knows nothing of her change of heart, only her kindness at Pemberley.

Mrs Bennet's bitterness towards Darcy, an example of uninformed prejudice, makes Elizabeth even more insecure.

Chapter 54, *pp. 273–6*

Elizabeth's reaction to Darcy's behaviour is sulky annoyance. Jane, though she denies it, is happy to have seen Bingley, and Elizabeth is sure their affection is unchanged.

Next week, at a party at Longbourn, Jane and Bingley's relationship improves further, but Elizabeth has no real opportunity to talk to Darcy and is embarrassed at her mother's coldness towards him. She realizes that Darcy's pride was probably so wounded by her first refusal that he will never make another offer. After the party, though Mrs Bennet is jubilant, Jane still refuses to admit that Bingley cares for her.

The suspense increases. Elizabeth is frustrated and annoyed at not being able to meet Darcy. She now admits his right not to be humiliated by rejection, and regrets having rejected him. Meanwhile, Jane and Bingley's romance develops easily and quickly.

Chapter 55, *pp. 277–82*

Darcy leaves for London. Bingley calls at Longbourn and is warmly welcomed; Jane now stops trying to hide her affection for him. The following day, Elizabeth finds the couple together, and it is obvious that Bingley has proposed and been accepted. Elizabeth, realizing that this is a worthy marriage, sees it as 'the happiest, wisest, most reasonable end' (p. 279). Mr Bennet comments that the couple are suited because they are both so easy-going, and Mrs Bennet is delighted to have yet another daughter engaged.

Jane tells Elizabeth that Bingley did not in fact know that she was in London during the spring. She now realizes that Caroline Bingley is responsible for this and learns a lesson: people are not necessarily as good as she would like to think them. Elizabeth does not admit the truth. She does, however, remark over Jane's happiness that she herself would be grateful to meet another Mr Collins – showing clearly how her views have developed since chapter 19.

Jane and Bingley are united in this chapter. As throughout their relationship, the proposal and engagement are romantic. The young girl accepts the dashing hero and is 'the happiest creature in the world' (p. 279). Their relationship is also quite unrealistic. As Mr Bennet says, it will succeed because they are both perfectly good-tempered. Conversely, Elizabeth, as she realizes, will never have Jane's happiness because she will never be the perfect romantic heroine. Notice her ironic acknowledgement that she will now be lucky to find a husband.

Chapter 56, *pp. 283–9*

A week after the engagement, Elizabeth receives an unexpected visit from Lady Catherine. She is patronizing, unfriendly and threatening, and this time there is nothing faintly comic about her behaviour. She has heard a rumour that Elizabeth is to marry Darcy, and officiously declares that she has plans for Darcy and Lady Anne to marry. Considering the Bennets' inferiority and Lydia's disgrace, a marriage with Elizabeth would be degrading.

Elizabeth refuses to be intimidated, saying she regards herself as equal to Darcy, and if he does not object to her connections, no one else should. Lady Catherine asks Elizabeth directly whether she is engaged to Darcy, and at her reply asks her not to accept his proposal. Elizabeth refuses and Lady Catherine leaves, saying she will have her own way. Of course, Elizabeth cannot tell anyone the reason for the visit.

Elizabeth has overcome almost every obstacle to a union with Darcy. Now she overcomes the representative of the superior Darcy aristocracy challenging her right to enter the family. Elizabeth correctly argues what she has always believed, and what Darcy himself now realizes (though she does not know this), that she herself is equal to Darcy, and if he does not care about social barriers, neither should she. In doing so, she does not convince Lady Catherine. Her victory lies in the fact that she stands up for herself as a person, she shows courage, argues rationally, and loves Darcy enough to fight for him. Again, although she does not know it, her behaviour encourages Darcy to propose a second time.

As well as revealing Elizabeth's character, we see here the epitome of false pride and prejudice caricatured in Lady Catherine's officious, stubborn nature. This is what Elizabeth must overcome if she is to be mistress of Pemberley.

Chapter 57, *pp. 290–93*

Elizabeth is concerned that Lady Catherine will turn Darcy against her. She knows that if he does not return to Longbourn, she will have lost him. Further doubts arise when her father receives a letter from Collins, congratulating him on Jane's engagement, but warning that acceptance of Darcy's proposal to Elizabeth will anger Lady Catherine. Her father's disbelieving reaction – 'his . . . indifference and your . . . dislike . . . make it . . . absurd' (p. 292) – makes her wonder if Darcy really does care for her. Collins closes with harsh condemnation of Lydia and the news that Charlotte is expecting a child.

This chapter contains Elizabeth's final trial: the doubts about her marriage expressed by her father, whose opinion she respects. These prove, in fact, that the appearance of a situation is not the reality, but they worry Elizabeth, who has now learnt that her judgement is not infallible. The news of Charlotte's condition puts the final seal of success on that particular marriage.

Chapter 58, *pp. 294–9*

Darcy returns to Netherfield and visits Longbourn with Bingley. During a walk, Elizabeth plucks up the courage to thank him for what he did for Lydia. He replies that 'I thought only of you', and then asks if she still feels as she did last April. Elizabeth immediately explains how much her feelings have changed and Darcy tells her of his love in a way that shows how genuine it is.

The remainder of the chapter contains Darcy's explanation of his actions since the first proposal and a discussion by both of their faults. Elizabeth admits how ashamed she now is of her actions and how through Darcy's letter, 'gradually all her former prejudices had been removed' (p. 296). Darcy then confesses how he took to heart Elizabeth's accusations of his ungentlemanly behaviour, how his childhood had raised him to be proud, and how grateful he is for Elizabeth's lesson. He explains that it was her reaction to Lady Catherine that showed him she might care for him. Finally, we learn that Darcy's visits to Longbourn made him aware that Jane did love Bingley, so he advised his friend to propose to her.

Everything in the book has been leading to this second proposal of Darcy's. You may be surprised then at how briefly it is described. Remember that the most important events in the book are the changes of heart Elizabeth and Darcy undergo. The proposal is merely an outward sign of their maturity and love. Notice, too, that when Jane Austen deals with true emotion, as here in a successful proposal, she does not intrude. She leaves us to imagine what was said.

We see clearly the change in Darcy and Elizabeth. Now, Darcy 'respects' (p. 295) Elizabeth's family, thinks 'only' (p. 295) of her, not himself, and receives Elizabeth's unexpected acceptance with both gratitude and happiness. Elizabeth is quick to admit that she is selfish, and she thanks him for his generosity, fully aware of how his pride must have been injured. Notice, too, how Elizabeth, whose life previously has been based on outward appearance, does not now look at Darcy as he proposes, but listens fully and correctly assesses his love.

Both have realized their faults, their pride and prejudice, their dependence on each other if they are to develop and grow, and their wish to make each other happy: a true sign of love. We are certain from their communication, respect and affection that the union will be a happy one.

Chapter 59, *pp. 300–305*

Elizabeth is worried about breaking the news to her family. Jane greets Elizabeth's statement as 'impossible' (p. 300) and is very concerned lest Elizabeth marry 'without affection' (p. 301), but Elizabeth soon convinces Jane of her true feelings for Darcy. Next day, Darcy again visits with Bingley, who now knows the news. That evening, Darcy asks Mr Bennet's consent. He gives it, but is also concerned lest, like his own marriage, Elizabeth's should be 'unequal' (p. 303), ending in discredit and misery.

Elizabeth assures her father 'I like him . . . I love him. He has no improper pride' (p. 303). Mr Bennet is then delighted, and when he learns of Darcy's generosity to Lydia, wryly comments that now he need not repay him.

Elizabeth here reconciles her family to the match, overcoming their prejudice. It is highly reminiscent of Charlotte's breaking the news of her engagement, an equally 'impossible' idea to Elizabeth. Notice how Elizabeth now understands Darcy's pride and defends it before her family. This defence, her standing up to her father's doubts, shows clearly that Elizabeth has grown up and at last shed the parental shackles.

Chapter 60, *pp. 306–9*

In a final conversation between Darcy and Elizabeth, Darcy comments that her spirit and kindness to Jane first attracted him. She argues that he loved her because she did not seek his approval. In a series of letters, Lady Catherine, Mrs Gardiner and Collins are told the news. When Lady Catherine hears the news the Collinses are forced to come to Lucas Lodge until her anger has abated. Caroline and Georgiana both write, with insincere and sincere congratulations respectively.

Darcy bears well with Elizabeth's family, but she now fully realizes the difference in quality between them, and cannot wait to be at Pemberley.

This chapter, like the next, completes the unfinished business in the book. We also hear of the reasons for Darcy's attraction from both Darcy and Elizabeth. Elizabeth prepares herself for the physical and mental transition to Pemberley.

Chapter 61, *pp. 310–12*

Darcy and Elizabeth, now married, go to Pemberley, and soon after Jane and Bingley join them in Derbyshire. These four 'good' characters move together into the adult, married world to find their own material and spiritual fulfilment.

Mr Bennet visits often and Kitty improves herself by doing the same. Mary stays at home with her mother and is happier without the competition of her sisters. Wickham and Lydia's relationship soon declines: Wickham's affection dies and Lydia benefits little from the marriage. Their lack of love is paralleled by a lack of money, though both Elizabeth and Darcy help financially.

Caroline Bingley realizes that she will do best to forget what has happened and to be friendly to everyone. Lady Catherine breaks off contact for a while, but is eventually reconciled. Georgiana loves Elizabeth dearly and learns much from her lively relationship with Darcy. The Gardiners are well loved by the hero and heroine they have united.

Characters

Elizabeth

Elizabeth Bennet is *Pride and Prejudice*. Whereas all the other characters contribute to the book, she is the reason for its existence. Her personality, her attitudes and her development bring together the story and all the characters.

Elizabeth's basic character is clear. She is an upper-middle-class woman, not yet twenty-one. She is, as we learn from Darcy's comments, attractive but not beautiful, with lovely eyes which show her intelligence and personality. She is clever, quick, lively, with an ability not only to see the humour in people and events, but also to laugh at herself.

Perhaps Elizabeth's most appealing characteristic is her independence, her 'self-sufficiency' (p. 221). She does not regulate her behaviour to please others, but judges things for herself, giving her firm opinion and acting on it. She can, in fact, be sharp-tongued and quite capable of teasing and challenging people. She acts decisively and, certainly at the start of the book, will not be made to change her mind, however great the emotional pressure. See, for example, how she quietly and calmly stands up to Mrs Bennet over Collins's proposal (p. 95). She argues at the end of the book, and is probably correct, that her self-sufficiency finally made Darcy fall in love with her (p. 306).

To offset this formidable strength of character, Elizabeth is also emotional. She feels great affection for Jane and is concerned about Lydia and Kitty. She has a surprisingly equal, warm relationship with her father, though she is exasperated by her mother. She is genuinely good-hearted and kind, actively so, not passively like Jane. She is firm friends with Charlotte and responds warmly and intuitively to

Georgiana's shyness. She even tries to let Collins down lightly, despite her aversion to him, and is willing for Lydia's sake to strike a truce with Wickham. Later she helps the couple with her own money. In short, she is a warm-hearted and emotional woman.

Unfortunately, all these positive qualities have their negative side. Elizabeth's self-sufficiency and lack of concern about the opinion of others can lead to problems when they conflict with society's rules. Mrs Bennet calls her 'wild' (p. 38) and Collins retreats when he hears she may be 'headstrong' (p. 93). Elizabeth's cleverness and strength of character, which we sense are unusual in her society, also give her a feeling of natural superiority. She, like her father and Darcy, knows she is more intelligent than others and she enjoys that. Elizabeth does not patronize Collins, for example, but she sees the difference between herself and the clergyman very clearly. In short, she suffers fools, but will always feel superior to them.

Her way of coping is to laugh at whatever she cannot accept or whatever threatens her; to laugh at adversity is better than sheltering behind one's pride, like Darcy, or sinking into despondency, like Jane. However, it has its dangers. Elizabeth tells Darcy she hopes she does not mock what is 'wise or good' (p. 50), but in fact she does just that. She mocks him, for she cannot otherwise cope with his superficial manner, and she does not look beyond it to see the real man.

This brings us to Elizabeth's main fault – prejudice. As Darcy is Pride, so Elizabeth is the Prejudice of the book's title. She may see and judge for herself, but unfortunately these judgements are often based on appearance rather than reality, on her strong emotions, not on rational thought.

The two main targets for Elizabeth's prejudice are Darcy and Wickham. She remarks that from the beginning she meant to be 'uncommonly clever' in disliking Darcy 'without any reason' (p. 185). In fact, her original dislike is seen as being justified. Darcy's first comment was cruel enough to offend. Afterwards, however, she delights in provoking him, and when he is denounced by Wickham, is more than ready to believe the accusations about him. One moment she is stating firmly that she does not think Darcy capable of such inhumanity, the next she is unequivocally accepting Wickham's story that he is!

From the start, Elizabeth is 'out of her senses' (p. 231) about Wickham's looks and charm, continually repeating to herself and Jane that his appearance means he must be telling the truth. Through twenty chapters (and Wickham's abandoning her for Miss King) she believes this, completely rejecting the evidence of his character offered by Jane, Mrs Gardiner and Caroline Bingley, all of whom, ironically, Elizabeth considers to be prejudiced.

Darcy's letter opens her eyes to the truth. He has already told her in the proposal that she only hears what she wants to hear. Being basically honest and aware, she tries to read his letter openly, and on the second reading does so, analysing it rationally to notice Wickham's inconsistencies and the lack of real evidence of his goodness.

Here, Elizabeth's viewpoint shifts, as she realizes how 'blind, partial, prejudiced' (p. 171) she has been. She also realizes that she is guilty of the same fault she accused Darcy of having – pride. She too has believed herself to be superior to others, clung to her opinions and refused to believe she is wrong, her vanity fuelled by Wickham's attentions and offended by Darcy's. She realizes that 'Till this moment, I never knew myself' (p. 171).

The actual shift in viewpoint is a sudden and emotional shock. It is a crucial moment, for Elizabeth and the novel, which marks her realization of her faults and her decision to change.

Although Elizabeth is still angry with Darcy, from this point on she is truly changed and, in the remainder of the book, she does try to see things clearly and without pride. She admits her faults to Jane, tells Wickham she knows the truth about him, tries to work out her problems honestly and rationally, and from now on values Darcy. It is her ability to do all this which make her the heroine of the novel. Faced with the truth about herself, realizing she has been badly affected by both her pride and her prejudice, she accepts the fact, thinks about it and acts on her conclusions. She has become a mature adult.

Along with her developing character, Elizabeth's views on love and marriage also change. Jane Austen uses Elizabeth to show us the mature, ideal marriage, and by contrasting through her eyes other, less worthy marriages, we ourselves learn what is best.

At first, Elizabeth is clear about what she expects from a relationship.

As she tells Charlotte, she is not seeking a husband, let alone a rich one. She despises courtship games, wants to know all about her partner, and when she hears of Charlotte's engagement, her reaction is 'impossible!' (p. 105). She slowly learns that her prejudice has led her astray. Hunsford shows her that such a marriage as Charlotte and Collins's is not only possible, but a fair compromise. Darcy's views, Pemberley, and the elopement show her too that financial and social considerations in marriage are important. She needs to learn this before she can take a realistic view of marriage as a social union and become the responsible mistress of Pemberley. Remember, however, that Elizabeth's view of marriage as an equal partnership is also valid. Her refusal of Collins is correct. She rejects his patronizing approach just as she rejects Darcy's condescension. Charlotte and Collins's marriage works because it is balanced, and Elizabeth too must meet her equal before a match will work.

What is Elizabeth's view of sexuality? She is as appalled as the rest, seeing the elopement as shameful, anti-social and irresponsible, and bound to be Lydia's downfall. However, Elizabeth also has the strength of character to question whether such a marriage is right; should respectability have to be purchased at the price of happiness?

Elizabeth's relationship with Wickham typifies romantic liaisons with their instant attraction, impractical emotion, and the idealization of the beloved. Jane Austen uses standard romantic terms to describe Elizabeth's preparation for the Netherfield ball to conquer 'all that remained unsubdued of his heart' (p. 76). Their relationship develops on the basis of Wickham's charm and Elizabeth's susceptibility, although she knows, as shown in her conversations with Mrs Gardiner, that it is a temptation, and that such a financially unstable marriage would not show 'wisdom' (p. 122). Upon Wickham's defection to his heiress, Elizabeth denies that she has been in love. Is she being honest? She continues to see Wickham as a model of goodness and to toy briefly with romance with a similar sort of man, Colonel Fitzwilliam, until Darcy's letter disillusions her. During her change of heart she abandons, along with her prejudice, her ideals about romance. She admits its validity in Jane's and Bingley's case, but only because they are perfectly good people. Elizabeth needs a real partner someone like Darcy.

You might like to decide for yourself the point at which Elizabeth falls in love with Darcy. The fact that she dislikes and provokes him in the early part of the book may well be a sign of her attraction, but Elizabeth does not admit it. She claims to find him obnoxious, and certainly has no second thoughts about refusing his first patronizing proposal. Even after the dawning of self-realization, she seems only to regret her actions and to be flattered by the proposal, and says she does not want to see Darcy ever again.

Not until her visit to Pemberley does Elizabeth appreciate Darcy's real worth and his change of heart, and she begins then to feel more for him; her view of marriage also begins to change. She soon realizes the justice of Darcy's accusations about her family, and Lydia's elopement only confirms this. The inequalities between her and Darcy are eventually overcome, and Elizabeth betters herself by marrying Darcy. Notice that she never takes advantage of this. Seeing Pemberley marks the start of her affection for Darcy because there she begins to appreciate his real character, rather than simply his wealth.

The elopement crystallizes Elizabeth's view on marriage – she now sees the ideal, and realizes that Darcy could provide it, 'answer' her needs (p. 252). His generosity on Lydia's behalf compounds her feelings and when he returns to Longbourn, Elizabeth is quiet and uncertain; he is now important to her and she knows that she needs his attention and approval.

Elizabeth's final test, having realized her own feelings, is to combat Darcy's family and her own. She defeats Lady Catherine first, defending the right of herself and Darcy to choose their own partners. Her courage unwittingly encourages Darcy to propose, although it is Elizabeth who opens the conversation by admitting her faults and confessing her needs. She then overcomes her own family's prejudice against Darcy, showing that she is now an independent adult and ready to be married.

Elizabeth's relationship with Darcy is sound. They communicate well, give each other mutual support and affection and generally complement each other. He will control her spirit by his rationality, and she will give him a less severe, more emotional view of the world. Elizabeth has found her true partner, with whom she can live at Pemberley, her true home.

At the end of the book, Elizabeth is the happy heroine, the centre of everything. She has not only changed herself through her love for Darcy, but has changed Darcy through his love for her. She has been responsible, in various ways, for all the marriages of her sisters, and through them has met her own match. She has found an inner maturity, now reflected by her outward adult status and marked by her forming her own family, united in love.

Darcy

What should the hero of a novel be like? Courteous, dashing, charming – in fact, nothing like Darcy! Yet he is the hero of *Pride and Prejudice*, and he is the right hero, a real person who is the hero first because he can change and mature and secondly because he is a true partner for the heroine, Elizabeth.

At first, however, Darcy seems to be the villain of the book. He appears at the Meryton ball and is immediately disliked by everyone because he so obviously disapproves of the evening, will not mix, and seems above himself, particularly to Elizabeth. What we learn about him later supports this view: he is 'haughty, reserved . . . continually giving offence' (p. 17). These impressions are strengthened by more serious criticisms: his condescending manner towards Elizabeth at Netherfield, his actions to Wickham, his influencing of Bingley against Jane.

By the end of chapter 33 we, like Elizabeth, have come to form a clear but negative view of Darcy. Then he proposes, but patronizingly, and they quarrel, gaining self-awareness shortly after. From this point on, Darcy ceases to be an anti-hero (the opposite of a hero) and begins to change. We also begin to view him differently.

Once the truth behind Wickham's assertions and the reasoning behind Darcy's influence of Bingley are known, Elizabeth begins to reconsider her opinion of Darcy. The business with Wickham was, of course, a slander. Darcy seems to have done all that could have been asked of him and more: to have judged Wickham correctly and to have been generous enough not to seek revenge for the planned elopement.

Over the Jane and Bingley affair, he seems to have acted honestly, if through pride, and his concern for Bingley's welfare is touching.

We, like Elizabeth, begin to see things in a new light, and to reconsider our own opinion of Darcy. Notice that in fact the very first impression he gave, at the Meryton ball, was good: 'fine, handsome, noble' (p. 12). We learnt too that he was intelligent and clear-sighted, and his conversations with Elizabeth certainly showed his thought and intelligence. When Elizabeth finally realizes that Darcy is right for her, she comments particularly on his 'judgement, information, and knowledge of the world' (p. 252).

We should be aware also of Darcy's real kindness and generosity. He is an affectionate brother, trusted by Georgiana, a wise and generous landlord and a good friend to Bingley. His free use of money to help first Wickham, then Lydia, is admirable.

In fact, Darcy's chief fault is his pride, and this he honestly tries to conquer in the course of the book. His is the pride in the title of the novel. He was brought up to be proud, almost trained to it. At the start of the book, he triumphantly defends it, though he realizes the importance of controlling it, which he feels he can do.

However, Darcy is wrong. His pride does lead him to behave wrongly – on three occasions. He conceals Wickham's faults because he does not wish the name of Darcy to be humiliated. He is totally convinced of his own good judgement over the matter of Jane and so influences Bingley accordingly. Over Elizabeth, his pride causes him to despise her family connections, and though at first he resists, the attraction remains; he sees his own proposal as demeaning, without realizing the implications of this for his love.

Elizabeth meets his proposal with genuine anger, and for the first time in his life Darcy's 'arrogance, conceit, disdain' (p. 160) are challenged. This is, of course, the point of change for Darcy. He afterwards tells Elizabeth that it took him some time to begin to alter, but in fact by the next morning, he has understood enough to want to justify himself in a letter. He thinks over his actions, slowly realizing 'how insufficient were all my pretensions to please a woman worthy of being pleased' (p. 297). By the time we reach Pemberley, he is eager to show his new persona. His outward manner, unlike so many in the book, is a sign of his inward change. He accepts Elizabeth and her relations, and soon after accepts responsibility for Lydia's elopement and arranges her marriage. His final proposal expresses his hopes, but not expectations, of being accepted, and he admits his pride, with gratitude to Elizabeth for humbling him.

We must not, however, judge Darcy too harshly. He is neither vain nor self-centred. Much of his pride is valid, the natural result of being master of Pemberley, affording him a self-confidence that allows him to help others. Equally, Elizabeth has coloured our view. Much of Darcy's pride is a figment of her own prejudice. Her final declaration to her father, that 'he has no improper pride', says everything (p. 303).

Although Darcy represents pride in the book, he is not without prejudice. He sees beyond superficial appearance more quickly than Elizabeth, but nevertheless dismisses her at first glance on her looks alone. He soon changes his mind but is still put off by her inferior connections and does not consider her on her true merits. He learns to reorganize his priorities after the rejection of the first proposal, and on his return to Longbourn is not disheartened by his reception, also seeing clearly now what he before judged wrongly – Jane's feelings for Bingley.

Darcy is, however, generally far more clear-sighted than the heroine, and points out to Elizabeth that she is prejudiced. This is the point of self-awareness for her, and completes the circle whereby both hero and heroine are responsible for the other's maturity.

Intermingled with the development of Darcy's character is the development of his love. He is, from the start, Elizabeth's obvious match; the story of their union is the story of the novel. At first he dismisses her, then is attracted by her 'playfulness' (p. 23) and her kindness to Jane. His love is immature, though, an infatuation he resists. Notice that his only comment on 'love' is a hackneyed reference to poetry (p. 40) which Elizabeth rightly dismisses. He feels 'bewitched' (p. 46), threatened, almost resentful of Elizabeth's power over him. For a while, rationality rules, then it is overcome by his emotions and he proposes.

He does so confidently, but with little real affection; the honest rebuff, as we previously commented, makes him stop, reassess what

Elizabeth thinks of him and act on it. At first, he is only concerned to live up to his 'gentlemanly' idea of himself in the future, but whilst trying to do this at Pemberley, he begins to develop a genuine regard for Elizabeth. Over the elopement, his emotional awareness and practical help both reflect and develop the growing affection he feels. One thing is certain: only when Darcy overcomes his faults and infatuation and acts truly for Elizabeth's sake can he hope to win her. When he does, also righting the wrong he has done, by persuading Bingley after all to marry Jane, he proposes again. He is now in a position to receive the 'happiness' (p. 295) he deserves.

You might like to think about the suggestion that Darcy's change of heart is too great and largely unexplained. Remember, though, that this is the first time Darcy has been truly in love, and that, because she is the right woman for him, Elizabeth is able to affect him deeply.

Darcys' and Elizabeth's is the one true union in the book. Darcy is good for Elizabeth; his pride shows her her own and through him she learns how prejudiced she is. He alone can stand up to her, balancing her uncontrolled emotion with his controlled rationality. He 'answers' (p. 252) her utterly, as no one else can.

Darcy is thus the hero. To ask, as we have done with other characters, whether he is important to the novel is as pointless as asking whether Elizabeth is. His worthiness contrasts clearly with all the other male characters in the book. Pompous Collins is the wrong side of Darcy's pride; Wickham's outward charm contrasts with Darcy's inner goodness; Mr Bennet's passivity shows us Darcy's active strength, and Bingley, though a true friend, reveals Darcy's strength by his own weakness.

His personality also contrasts with Elizabeth's, complementing it, as has been said, and forming a true unity. As her partner, complement and male equivalent, Darcy is as much the centre of the book as Elizabeth, though it is not seen through his eyes. He represents the male ideal: intelligence, rationality, good judgement and right action, has a handsome, moneyed appearance but is nevertheless valued for his true, inner qualities. He also represents the male side of the love relationship, a mature, strong affection which considers the other before itself.

Lydia

For the first two-thirds of the book, we actually hear very little about Lydia. She chases officers, teases Bingley about a ball and snubs Mr Collins. We see a well-developed, attractive girl whose sole interests are clothes, dancing and men. She is loud and forward, with a strong will and a self-confidence approaching rudeness, and she does not seem to care what others think, so long as she has their attention.

She does care what men think of her though, for they are the centre of her life. She and Kitty 'hang around' Meryton spotting various handsome officers, dancing with them at balls and storing up gossip about them. Lydia's affection for the officers is as a 'crush', the very opposite of real friendship or love; she does not know any of the soldiers as people but falls for the image and appearance of the soldier.

It is this, of course, that makes her easy prey for Wickham. The story of the elopement begins when Elizabeth returns to Longbourn (ch. 39), already having doubts about Lydia's behaviour because of Darcy's comments (p. 175). Jane Austen now focuses on Lydia in preparation for the elopement, devoting a whole chapter to Lydia's gossip. We see her as really silly. She has no idea about money or how to use it; she buys a hat she herself admits is ugly and enjoys silly games which make her giggle (pp. 180–83).

Elizabeth is at this stage seriously worried about Lydia, and when she learns of the forthcoming visit to Bath, is concerned at what will happen, fearing Lydia will be a ridiculous, 'determined flirt' (p. 190). Elizabeth is not simply saying that Lydia will enjoy men's company – she is making a serious criticism about Lydia's becoming dependent on the admiration she receives and therefore not responsible for her actions. Notice Lydia's ideas about Brighton on pp. 190–91. They reflect perfectly Elizabeth's fears.

In Brighton the worst happens. In Jane Austen's day, a girl was unmarriageable if she had eloped, and, once her parents were dead, was possibly without means of support. Lydia falls for Wickham without considering this, let alone the family disgrace. Her sense of fun, her stubbornness, and her sheer ignorance of Wickham's real nature and her own actions all make her an easy conquest. Elizabeth comments that she cannot see any reason why Wickham should marry Lydia, but every reason why he should seduce her (p. 227). However, Lydia is not a knowing mistress. Her note and her conversation with Mrs Gardiner show that she expected marriage; for all her faults, Lydia is simply a naïve child.

When Lydia returns to Longbourn (ch. 51), she has all that her mother has brought her up to want: a handsome husband, a wedding ring and married status. She giggles and patronizes her sisters until she leaves, and we can see that, unlike Elizabeth, she has learnt nothing from her love relationship. Her marriage to Wickham is characterized by a lack of money which reflects their growing lack of affection, and her letter to Elizabeth in chapter 61 shows that she is still as impudent and thoughtless as ever.

Lydia is not a likeable character, though she may have a great deal of our sympathy. She is self-centred, rude, and shows little real kindness for anyone. She is, though, a sad character. She is both ignorant and innocent of love and life, and her early marriage means that she never has the opportunity to learn better. Lydia is condemned to a life with a man who does not love her, and we can imagine her, like her mother, a pitiful figure in later life, though still retaining 'the claims to reputation which her marriage had given her' (p. 311).

Lydia is important to the book. First, of all the women, she is the one most ruled by sensation and the charm of appearances. She has 'animal spirits' (p. 40) – you cannot even say passion, for that suggests more depth and emotion than Lydia is capable of. To Jane Austen this is one aspect of womanhood – the allowing of passing sensation, fun and flirtation, attraction and attention to rule your life – and Lydia represents this. She is in many ways the opposite of every other woman in the book: quiet, controlled Jane, practical Charlotte, clever Caroline. Above all, she is the opposite of the heroine Elizabeth, whose awareness, intelligence and sensitive approach allow her not only to gain a good, stable relationship but also to mature, neither of which Lydia ever does.

However, in many ways, Lydia shows us what Elizabeth might have been. They have the same mother, once just as attractive and silly as Lydia, the same easy-going father. They are sisters, and Lydia's stubbornness, her wildness and her love of laughter are all found to a lesser degree in Elizabeth. Their dependence on outward opinion and openly expressed admiration is also similar, and when Wickham elopes with Lydia, surely Elizabeth might have thought 'There, but for Darcy's letter and my own strength of mind, go I . . .'

As well as representing the 'shallow woman', Lydia is also part of the shallow marriage. Her elopement is important at various levels. It affects the outcome of the book, bringing Elizabeth and Darcy – and thus Jane and Bingley – together. At the same time, the marriage is a parallel to Lydia's character, based on desire, sensation ruling thought, an anti-social union because it is essentially for personal pleasure, 'fun', without rational thought for the social consequences. The failure of Lydia's marriage at the end of the book is Jane Austen's final condemnation of her and what she represents.

Wickham

It is strange but true that rogues are often attractive. Wickham is a charmer, a handsome man who knows how to please people, especially women. He is gentle, has a 'captivating softness' (p. 149), a pleasant manner, and even when Elizabeth tells him to his face that she knows all he has done, he kisses her hand! Even his misdeeds have style: he lies plausibly, gambles with impunity, seduces young women easily. We can see, as we are meant to, why Elizabeth is taken in.

Like Elizabeth, however, we must think logically about Wickham. He is ruled solely by self-interest. His charm only shows itself to get him what he wants. He has, in his short life, cheated a great deal of money out of Darcy, attempted to take his revenge viciously by eloping with Darcy's sister, gambled away a small fortune, cold-bloodedly set out to marry into money and eloped yet again. Bribed into marrying, he is unable to sustain affection for long and degenerates into a poor and indifferent husband.

It is interesting that for someone who seems to be so active, affecting so many people's lives, Wickham actually appears very seldom in the book. His confrontation with Darcy and the subsequent revelations to Elizabeth are followed only by two short, if significant, conversations with Elizabeth, the reported elopements and a brief welcome and farewell at Longbourn.

His major role in the book is to help us understand Elizabeth, and to change her by her realization of what he is. He is, first, a potential suitor. At one point in the book (ch. 26) she would willingly have married him. In this way, Wickham shows us Elizabeth's romantic side, as well as providing a rival for Darcy. Notice that only for Wickham does Elizabeth have the classic romantic symptoms; only for him does she dress up, prepared for the 'conquest' (p. 76).

Of course, Wickham is the man to stir up these emotions, for he treats women in the standard romantic way, making them feel wanted, respected, admired – at first. Elizabeth learns, however, that at best he is a chauvinist. His treatment of her – dropping her for Mary King and expecting her to be available on his return – provokes her righteous anger. It soon becomes apparent that Wickham has a deeper disrespect for women which he uses to further his own ends. He uses Georgiana for money and revenge, Lydia for pleasure. In the end, Elizabeth sees both the man and the response he inspires as being worthless. Women who fall for such men are deceived.

Wickham also shows us Elizabeth's capacity for prejudice. The key scene occurs in chapter 14, where, on first acquaintance, Wickham pours out his self-pitying tale about Darcy. He is careful to test the strength of Elizabeth's bias first, then presents a clever story designed to stir sympathy and belief. Elizabeth is taken in completely. Wickham plays on her credulity, twisting the essential truth so that he appears in the best light and Darcy as proud and in the wrong.

Many of the other characters are equally taken in. Mrs Bennet and Lydia never see Wickham's true worthlessness, Jane admires him, and even Mrs Gardiner is impressed by his superficial appearance, though she suspects his inner one. In addition to showing personal blindness, Wickham also demonstrates public prejudice. Everyone agrees he is charming until the elopement, when they just as unanimously condemn him.

Although not directly because of Wickham, it is through him that

Elizabeth, realizing the truth of his vicious nature in chapter 36, also realizes her own lack of good judgement, her prejudice, her susceptibility to flattery. She sees the difference between appearance and reality, and this is clearly shown in her two further conversations with him (pp. 191–2, 263–5). In many ways, Wickham does Elizabeth a service by helping to teach her the main lesson of the book.

In many ways too, Wickham teaches Darcy his lesson, for whilst at first responding to Wickham regardless of the consequences for others, Darcy gradually learns to react without pride, and abandons his self-interest entirely when working for the benefit of Lydia's marriage. In the end, Darcy's love for Elizabeth is proved by his entering the Bennet family regardless of the fact that Wickham is a member, his pride now quite overcome.

Wickham's marriage is vital to the plot not only because it brings Elizabeth and Darcy together, but because it also represents what is in the end the wrong sort of marriage. For Wickham, more than for Lydia, it is a sexually-based relationship. He takes her to London for companionship, with no intention of marrying her. This is the truly anti-social act – placing sex before affection, knowing it may destroy the other person. Wickham ultimately submits to marriage because he is paid. The relationship has to fail for it is based, like Wickham's own character, on wrong.

To summarize then, Wickham represents the worthless man. Lydia is merely silly, but Wickham is vicious. Darcy's housekeeper calls him 'wild' (p. 202) and, like a wild animal, he is truly anti-social, against what society stands for, without an ability to love. He reflects, in his emotional irrationality, the weakest aspects of Elizabeth's character and stands in direct opposition to Darcy. It is ironic then that he should ultimately bring them together.

Jane

Jane, Elizabeth's sister, may seem too good to be true: she is kind, sweet-tempered and perfectly beautiful. Nevertheless, Jane Austen hints that Elizabeth occasionally feels just as exasperated by Jane as we might. On a few occasions, Elizabeth criticizes her sister for her good nature, and an unrealistic inability to see the worst in people which amounts to prejudice. When, in chapter 55, Jane realizes Caroline Bingley's true character and criticizes her for it, Elizabeth is delighted, as are we, at this development in her character.

With Bingley, Jane represents romantic love, which is seen in the novel as unrealistic and suspect. It is Jane's sweet nature, hiding her vulnerability, which leads to her being misunderstood and losing Bingley for a while, with all the consequences on Darcy'and Elizabeth's relationship. Through Darcy all is resolved, but we still see that it is only because Jane is so good a person that her romantic relationship works, and, even so, it is less valid than Elizabeth and Darcy's tempestuous liaison.

However, we must not be too hard on Jane. She is a good and affectionate friend to Elizabeth, acting as confidante and helping her work through her problems. She is a dutiful and supportive daughter, takes full responsibility for the family during Lydia's elopement, and is the special favourite of the Gardiner children.

Jane is also a contrast to Elizabeth. Her passive nature – she hardly does anything in the novel which is not initiated by someone else – is the opposite of Elizabeth's self-sufficiency. Her unquestioning approval of everything shows us clearly the critical prejudice and the pride in Elizabeth's nature. Despite her unrealistic viewpoint, she several times is proved right about matters that Elizabeth's stubborn opinion had declared to be 'impossible'. Of course, she also complements Elizabeth, as Bingley does Darcy. At the end of the book, it is Jane and Bingley who join the hero and heroine in Derbyshire as true friends and 'good' characters.

Bingley

Jane's partner, Bingley, is her equal in every way, a good-tempered, passive, easily influenced man. Bingley is handsome, rich and charming. He and Jane become more and more attracted to each other. When they separate, he is genuinely regretful; once they are reunited, we have Mr Bennet's opinion and Elizabeth's belief that he and Jane are ideally suited and the marriage is the 'happiest, wisest, most reasonable end' (p. 279).

Despite all this, Bingley is a character with faults. Like Jane, he approves of everything and everyone indiscriminately, is arbitrarily enthusiastic, and is so easily influenced that he abandons true affection on the advice of a friend, but is as easily advised into marriage. His friendship with Darcy is based on admiration and dependence, though remember that, like Jane, he complements Darcy, offsetting the latter's critical, off-putting manner.

Bingley never himself influences the progress of the book, though his leaving of Jane – initiated by Darcy – affects Elizabeth, Jane and Darcy himself. Instead, he acts as a foil to Darcy, showing his character by contrast, highlighting Wickham's false charm by his own genuine kindness, showing us Elizabeth's character through her view, and defence, of him.

Bingley also shows us the negative side of romantic love. Though Elizabeth defends Bingley, Mrs Gardiner's criticisms (pp. 119–20) are true, and show us that real love is stable, developing and realistic. We see from this the true worth of Darcy and Elizabeth's relationship.

Collins

From his first letter, Collins is recognized by Elizabeth, Mr Bennet and ourselves as a humorous figure who is also stupid, pompous and conceited.

He enters the book first as a suitor for Elizabeth. He is obviously unsuitable, but he clarifies the reasons for her attraction to Wickham, and, when he proposes, shows clearly her views on marriage, acting as a contrast to Darcy's later proposals. As a suitor, just as a person, Collins leaves a lot to be desired. His reasons for marrying are selfish, he humiliates Elizabeth even while proposing, and he lacks the sensitivity to realize her refusal is genuine. This scene is comic, but nevertheless has a worrying aspect.

However, when his reasons for marrying are matched by those of

Charlotte, who is equally practical, a good relationship results. Elizabeth learns from this one of the most important lessons of the book: that her horror at the thought of such a marriage is misplaced. The Hunsford visit, as well as allowing for Darcy's first proposal, teaches her that such a match can work, preparing her for the more realistic approach to marriage which comes with maturity.

As a clergyman, Collins is less than perfect. Jane Austen strongly satirizes clergymen such as Collins and Elton (in *Mansfield Park*) who both condescend to make time to serve their parish and who – as we see in Collins's letter to Mr Bennet over the elopement – have precious little Christian charity.

Collins is also a caricature of pride. His background has given him a servile manner, and the patronage of Lady Catherine has made him conceited. He uses shallow flattery to hide his basically patronizing attitude to everyone, even Darcy. He sees himself as all-important, even when love is involved; only 'his pride was hurt' (p. 95) by Elizabeth's rejection.

Collins's final purpose in the novel is to highlight, by comparison, the faults in Darcy's first proposal, but also to show by contrast why Darcy's goodness makes him, not Collins, the right partner for Elizabeth.

The Gardiners

Mr Gardiner is a sensible man, in trade but nevertheless a gentleman. He is more able to handle Lydia's elopement than is her own father.

Mrs Gardiner is both a friend and a mother to Elizabeth. She judges Bingley's affection, warns Elizabeth to distrust violent emotion (p. 119) and helps by removing Jane to London. She also warns Elizabeth against an unwise marriage with Wickham, and criticizes his courtship of Mary King.

By taking Elizabeth with them to Pemberley, the Gardiners advance her relationship with Darcy. He is impressed by them at Pemberley, thus increasing his respect for Elizabeth. The Gardiners correctly assess Darcy's love for Elizabeth and tactfully encourage it. They are the 'good parents' that Elizabeth lacks and to a large extent are the means of uniting her with Darcy.

Caroline Bingley

Bingley's sister is a disagreeable character. She is a clear example of social pride and class prejudice arising out of her own beauty, riches and education. Jane Austen faults Caroline for her snobbery, for her wish to marry Darcy and the ways she tries to win him, her jealousy of Elizabeth, and her interference in Jane and Bingley's relationship.

As the typical marriage-minded woman, Caroline also presents another useful contrast to Elizabeth. She is also a potential rival to the heroine at Netherfield, and when Elizabeth visits Pemberley and overcomes Caroline's viciousness by her calm control and protection of Georgiana, she not only wins Darcy's increased affection, but overcomes yet another obstacle to her union with him.

Lady Catherine de Bourgh

Lady Catherine de Bourgh is Darcy's aunt and Collins's patroness. A caricature of pride and social prejudice, she derives pleasure in life from controlling others and proving her superiority, often with humorous effect. She adds substance to Wickham's claims of the Darcy pride by demonstrating it, shows Collins's pride through his reaction to her, and contrasts Darcy's good pride with her bad.

Lady Catherine's main purpose in the book is to show Elizabeth's character, first when Elizabeth stands up to her at Rosings and later at Longbourn. The final challenge to Elizabeth's love is Lady Catherine's demand that she give up Darcy, which allows Elizabeth to prove her worth by refusing, thus defeating pride and prejudice combined in the character of Lady Catherine, and the symbol of Darcy's superiority. This also brings Darcy and Elizabeth together by encouraging Darcy to propose.

Charlotte Lucas

Charlotte, Elizabeth's friend, is described as 'sensible, intelligent' (p. 18). She has always seen the necessity for a practical marriage, and knows how to achieve it by encouraging a man, just as she encourages Collins. She makes the relationship work, at the same time retaining her emotional independence. The lesson of Charlotte's marriage teaches Elizabeth as nothing else can that practical considerations are both important to, and possible in, a marriage, a realization that is vital before Elizabeth can marry Darcy.

Charlotte is a good friend to Elizabeth; upset at her reaction to the marriage with Collins, she pursues the friendship and invites Elizabeth to Hunsford. This allows Darcy and Elizabeth to meet, leads to the proposal, and paves the way for the self-awareness that follows. Charlotte also acts as a contrast to Elizabeth, in her practical and rational attitude to life.

Mr Bennet

Elizabeth's father is one of the more likeable characters in the book. His goodness shows in the real affection he feels for Elizabeth, his sensitivity in his comments to Elizabeth over her true worth (p. 190) and her marriage to Darcy (pp. 303–4).

Conversely, he and his wife form one example of a physically-based marriage, now inevitably failed. His answer is to be philosophical, laughing at annoyances and withdrawing from responsibility. He is a poor family man; his mockery of Mrs Bennet is humiliating and erodes the children's respect; he has no financial sense, and his weakness in letting Lydia go to Brighton has terrible results.

He plays little part in the book, apart from allowing Lydia to go to Brighton, but his contribution is humorous and genuinely worthwhile.

Mrs Bennet

Mrs Bennet is a caricature of the matchmaking mother. Her wish for husbands for her daughters colours her view of everything, and makes her behave badly – notice her vicious comments to Elizabeth over the Collins proposal, her resentment of Charlotte's marriage, her delight, heedless of the disgrace to the family, over Lydia and Wickham's wedding.

She is a humorous figure, providing light relief by her continual chatting and gullibility. She exemplifies for us a figure in a failed marriage based on early sexual attraction. She also affects the action of the book by unwittingly convincing Darcy that marriage between Bingley and Jane would be a mistake; his final acceptance of her is a true triumph of love over pride and prejudice.

Commentary

Pride

If we say people are proud, we mean they see themselves as being superior to others, convinced they are important and right in everything they do. Pride, like prejudice, is a vice in society because proud people are always seeking what they see as their just reward, often at others' expense. They are unwilling to help those they consider their inferiors, they are always patronizing others. Most of all, their conceit prevents them from developing their own personalities.

In *Pride and Prejudice*, Jane Austen looks at people who are guilty of pride, and the effects it has both on their lives and on the lives of others. Everyone in the book has some degree of pride, but the key characters are first the caricatures of proud people: Collins, and Lady Catherine; and secondly, those who are developed characters with pride as a part of their personality: Darcy and Elizabeth.

Caricatured pride is straightforwardly obnoxious. Lady Catherine is proud because she was born an aristocrat, raised to believe herself superior to others. Notice how she is bringing up her condescending daughter in the same way. She is patronizing, believes she has a right to know and judge everything, and gives petty advice because she needs to feel useful. She always likes to be the centre of attention, and she expects always to be obeyed.

Lady Catherine is challenged by Elizabeth who, unlike almost everyone else, is not overawed by her. Lady Catherine is outraged when Elizabeth answers her back at Rosings (p. 138), and even more so when she visits Longbourn and Elizabeth refuses to reject Darcy's offer (p. 287). Look particularly at this scene, where she first orders Elizabeth not to marry Darcy, then accuses her of ingratitude, and finally insults her by saying that accepting Darcy will pollute the shades of Pemberley (p. 288). That Elizabeth does not submit severely damages Lady Catherine's pride. She needs instant submission and gratitude.

Collins meets this need. He had been raised with 'humility of manner' (p. 61), but the good fortune of the Hunsford living has made him a mixture of 'pride and obsequiousness, self-importance and humility' (p. 61). Lady Catherine does not need to hide her pride to maintain her position but Collins does, and this servility makes him even more unlikeable.

Collins too needs to be the centre of attention, using flattery and Lady Catherine's reflected glory to gain this. He also enjoys putting other people down, as his self-righteous comments on Lydia's elopement show (pp. 240, 293). Perhaps the key scene showing Collins's pride is his proposal to Elizabeth, where he not only assures her he will not despise her for being without a dowry, but tells her that she might as well accept him, for he is the best she can expect. He then totally ignores her refusal, considering that no one could fail to want him. When he does understand, only 'his pride [is] hurt' (p. 95) and he sulks until Charlotte's flattering attention heals his wounds.

Elizabeth herself, though chiefly signifying prejudice, is guilty of the pride on which this prejudice is based. Darcy tells her when he proposes 'Had not your pride been hurt . . . [my faults] might have been overlooked' (p. 159), and in the key chapter that follows, she admits this. She has been convinced she was right about Bingley's treatment of Jane (p. 100), Charlotte and Collins's marriage (p. 105), Wickham's goodness and Darcy's lack of worth (p. 73). She learns that her prejudice has been due to her belief in the infallibility of her own judgement. Also, she realizes her vanity has been wounded.

The distinction between pride and vanity is made early in the book. Mary comments that 'Pride relates more to our opinion of ourselves, vanity to what we would have others think of us' (p. 20). As well as pride, Elizabeth has been guilty of vanity. She has been far too influenced by Wickham's attentions and Darcy's neglect. She admits this immediately, making an honest effort from then on to be neither proud nor vain (p. 171). Does she succeed?

The chief representative of pride is Darcy. On his introduction in chapter 3, he is said to be proud. He seems withdrawn, superior and cynical. He puts Elizabeth down coldly with a patronizing comment about her looks. Later, despite his infatuation, he feels himself superior to Elizabeth, and kindly condescends to ignore her towards the end of the Netherfield visit so that 'nothing could elevate her with the hope' of marrying above herself (p. 52). Pride convinces Darcy he is right to interfere in Bingley's relationship with Jane, and pride keeps him from lowering himself and his family by disclosing Wickham's bad nature.

By the time of the first proposal to Elizabeth, Darcy is firmly established as the epitome of pride. The proposal, 'not more eloquent on the subject of tenderness than of pride' (p. 157), reveals a Darcy who considers he is doing Elizabeth a favour. She is outraged, and accuses him of 'arrogance' and 'conceit' (p. 160).

Were Darcy a lesser character, he would, like Collins, have sulked and turned elsewhere, but Darcy, the hero, ponders Elizabeth's accusations, realizes their truth and resolves to change. We only see his outward alteration, his gentle behaviour at Pemberley, his assistance to the Bennets over the elopement. After the successful proposal, however, Darcy explains his change of heart. Loving Elizabeth has made him realize that people can be good despite their humble stations, and that love is not compatible with condescension.

Has Darcy turned, then, from being 'all pride' at the start of the book to all humility at the end? The answer must be no. First, Darcy is never all pride. Our view of him as such is largely formed by Elizabeth's prejudice. Also, Darcy is not guilty of every form of pride. He does not always seek reward or constant attention; in fact his reputation for pride, like Georgiana's, is largely due to the fact that he is shy and dislikes socializing. He may put people down, but he also helps them, as friends or dependants. Remember his housekeeper's kindly comments: 'Some people call him proud; but I am sure I never saw any thing of it' (p. 204).

By the end of the book, Darcy still has some pride, but with good reason. The mature Elizabeth has learnt, as have we, that there is good pride and bad. 'Vanity is a weakness' says Darcy, but with 'superiority of mind, pride will always be under good regulation' (p. 51). Elizabeth, thinking he is guilty of both, smiles. But Darcy is right. Vanity, as seen in Lady Catherine, Collins, Elizabeth, and even Darcy himself, is wrong, but pride, whilst also being essentially wrong, can be acceptable if properly controlled. In many ways, Darcy controls his pride. In the end, having cast off his vanity and destructive pride, his good pride, his legitimate self-esteem, is still intact. The Darcy who saves Lydia and marries Elizabeth has a regulated, socially acceptable self-confidence and self-esteem based on reason. Elizabeth realizes this after the first proposal. Pemberley reveals Darcy's social superiority. He is master of Pemberley by right and his pride in it is a natural product of upbringing and strength of character. Elizabeth becomes aware that rationally based pride is a positive attribute, bringing with it self-awareness and a capacity to help others – his family, tenants, friends. She also knows that rationally based pride can improve a person by instilling in him an honest desire to do good. Eventually, defending Darcy, Elizabeth tells her father that he is proud, but has 'no improper pride' (p. 303).

We see then that vanity – that self-centred concern about the opinion of others – is wrong, as is also the inflated self-opinionation that characterizes false pride. The faults of those caricatures of pride, Collins and Lady Catherine, do not alter in the course of the book. Darcy and Elizabeth, however, shed their bad qualities, retaining a rightful pride (or self-esteem), and use it for the good of the individual and society.

Prejudice

Prejudice, Jane Austen tells us in Elizabeth's key comment in chapter 36 (p. 171), is the fault of being blind to the truth because we are partial, of seeing appearance, not reality, because we have an interest in doing so. The reasons for prejudice may vary. We may be prejudiced towards someone because they please us or against someone because they reject us.

From the start of the book, Jane Austen talks of universal acknowledgement (p. 51), where society itself takes a united (and, she infers, biased) stand, welcoming Bingley because he is eligible, rejecting Darcy because he seems proud and favouring Wickham because he flatters and charms.

Against this general background of public prejudice, Jane Austen presents several particular illustrations of people who confuse appearance with reality because of their inner bias.

Mrs Bennet is probably the most humorous example of this, seeing the world in terms of the wealth and charm of potential husbands. Thus she is blind to Collins's faults, is deceived by Wickham, and yet cannot see Darcy's real worth: 'I hate the very sight of him' (p. 269). Though her reaction is so exaggerated that it seems funny, there is something very worrying about the way, for example, that Mrs Bennet welcomes Wickham as Lydia's husband, totally forgetting that he would have ruined the girl.

Jane, too, confuses appearance with reality. Her prejudice is caused by a natural instinct, so should not be too harshly criticized, as she is often right in her judgements. However, we get the impression that Jane Austen sees Jane's view of people as unrealistic and unbalanced, too good to be true, based on a desire for peace of mind which she gains by seeing everyone except herself as totally blameless (p. 116). So she swallows Caroline's tales, insincerity and mockery, blames herself for caring too much for Bingley, and still thinks well of Wickham, even when she learns of his elopement with Lydia. However, when in chapter 55 Jane realizes Caroline's true nature and speaks harshly of her, she has actually learned something at last. Unlike Mrs Bennet's, her prejudice can be changed, and we, like Elizabeth, say 'Good girl' (p. 281).

There is a core of social prejudice dealt with in the book which overlaps considerably with the vice of pride: social snobbery in those who bolster their vanity by regarding their social inferiors as being below them. Collins, Lady Catherine and the Bingley sisters all fail to see the real Bennets when they judge them early on. Look at Collins's proposal and how he constantly reminds Elizabeth of her inferior position in life, echoing the comments of Lady Catherine at Rosings. The Bingley sisters spend several sessions judging Jane and Elizabeth on their relatives and their wealth.

Darcy, though in the main clear-sighted and intelligent in his approach to life, at first joins in this social snobbery. His initial opinion of Elizabeth herself was formed by her lack of beauty, and then compounded by her lack of connections. His social prejudice led him to influence Bingley away from Jane and to resist his own infatuation for Elizabeth. His bias also stopped him from seeing Jane's real feelings about Bingley, though they were well hidden. It is only when Elizabeth points out his pride in the proposal that he realizes how it has clouded the 'impartial conviction' (p. 163) he considers he has. From then on he makes an honest effort to see clearly and to change his behaviour to reflect this. By the end of the book, he respects Elizabeth's family and sees only the true Elizabeth, not her social standing.

It is Elizabeth who most typifies prejudice for us. The first time she and Darcy meet he snubs her and this turns her against him. From then on, instead of attempting to understand him, she reacts only to his proud outer appearance, and delights in fuelling her prejudice as much as possible. At first, she can be pardoned for disliking a man who has insulted her but, as she admits, her reasons were not sound. She wanted to score points, to seem clever, and to say something witty.

The real development of prejudice comes in Elizabeth's conversation with Wickham in chapter 16. Whereas with Darcy an insult clouds her judgement, with Wickham it is sexual attraction and flattery that do so. She is, as she later admits, 'out of her senses' (p. 231), not thinking clearly when she accepts almost unquestioningly everything Wickham says about the Darcy family. At first, indeed, she states that she had not thought Darcy 'so bad as this' (p. 69), but a few lines later she is finding evidence of her own to support Wickham's claims, and in no time is totally convinced about the truth of his words.

It is not until the first proposal that Elizabeth doubts for a moment her judgements: then Darcy accuses her of being susceptible to flattery and 'disguise' (p. 159). The crucial chapter 36, where Elizabeth considers Darcy's letter, is a careful account of how her prejudice is overcome. At first absolutely biased against Darcy, without 'any wish of doing him justice' (p. 168), she then realizes that if his account is true, she must have deceived herself. Notice how, by putting the letter away she literally refuses to see the truth. Almost immediately, however, her strength of character triumphs. She rereads the letter, allowing rationality to overcome the flattery and insult that have over-burdened her emotions in a sound appraisal of its contents. She remembers how influenced she was by Wickham's appearance, the lack of evidence of his worth, the inconsistencies in his behaviour, and how the story of the planned elopement was confirmed by Colonel Fitzwilliam's reaction.

As quickly as she was deceived, Elizabeth now sees the situation clearly. She admits to being 'blind, partial, prejudiced' (p. 171) and achieves insight into the situation and her own character. She admits her fault to Jane, and by letting Wickham know that she sees the difference between appearance and reality (p. 192), she makes a public statement of her new self-knowledge, as well as going some way to correcting her previously prejudiced actions.

Apart from protecting Wickham by not revealing his true character (how far is this prejudiced?), Elizabeth sees clearly from now on, viewing Pemberley with unbiased eyes and meeting Darcy with an open mind. She also begins to understand his criticisms of her family, seeing them objectively possibly for the first time in her life. Finally, she comes to appreciate the justification of their union, as Darcy has always done, and fights to overcome her own family's prejudice against him by presenting him in his true light.

Elizabeth and Darcy struggle to gain their unbiased viewpoint. Is there evidence in the book of other similarly unprejudiced attitudes? Perhaps very little. Almost everyone has their blind spots. Charlotte sees clearly Jane's character and Darcy's infatuation, but Bingley refuses to be prejudiced when others snobbishly criticize the Bennets.

It is Mr Bennet who, though in many ways blind to the truth, shows he has true, if idealistic, vision when he tells Elizabeth that good people such as she and Jane will always be valued for themselves alone, not their status or wealth (p. 190). Unfortunately, he is wrong. People should be unprejudiced or, as Elizabeth and Darcy are, finally willing to learn to see the reality of true worth, not the appearance of it. However, as Jane Austen points out to us in *Pride and Prejudice*, what people should do and what they actually do are often very different.

Marriage

Marriage is the focal point of *Pride and Prejudice*. The plot concerns a series of marriages, the characters are revealed and developed through marriage and the lessons Jane Austen teaches us are centred around marriage.

Why should Jane Austen choose marriage as her main theme? In her world, both financially and socially, marriage was a woman's chief aim. Financially, because of women's dependent position, marriage was the 'only honourable provision' (p. 103), infinitely preferable to the dependency of spinsterhood or the near slave-labour of being a governess. Socially, it marked maturity. When she married and started a family, a woman took her place in society. So marriage is obviously the focus of interest in Jane Austen's world.

How does Jane Austen present her view? Against a background of conventional contemporary attitudes on the subject, she places a series of actual and possible relationships. Elizabeth and Darcy, Jane and Bingley, Lydia and Wickham all marry. Some couples, such as the Bennets, are already married, and there is a variety of potential marriages throughout the book. Through all of these Jane Austen shows us, and Elizabeth, what she considers to be worthwhile in marriage and life. Elizabeth eventually reaches a real understanding of what a good marriage involves, and she finds it with Darcy.

One model of marriage in Jane Austen's time was that of a business contract, joining and strengthening families' wealth and status, linking estates, providing heirs, giving women financial security. Partners were chosen for what might now seem unemotional reasons: fortune and connections similar to, but preferably better than, one's own.

At first, Jane Austen seems to disapprove strongly of such arrangements. From the opening sentence of the book, she mocks the link between marriage and money made by Mrs Bennet when talking about Bingley. Wickham's fortune-hunting is condemned by Mrs Gardiner; his eventual marriage, the result of a bribe (p. 263), is doomed from the start. Darcy's awareness of the 'inferiority of [Elizabeth's] connections' (p. 159) is seen as a major flaw in his character. All those who scheme for arranged financial marriages are condemned: Mrs Bennet, Lady Catherine, Caroline Bingley.

From the start, Elizabeth despises those who wed to be 'well married' (p. 22). She defends before Mrs Gardiner her right to marry without a fortune, and implies the same to Collins when he proposes. She is determined to choose her husband for love, rather than money. Jane Austen's judgement seems quite clear.

But Elizabeth must learn that she is partially wrong, that practical considerations are, in fact, vital to a good marriage. Without financial stability, in Jane Austen's world, people literally starved to death, and the building of a family circle with a sound economic base was therefore highly important. For example, Collins wishes to marry for his own 'happiness' (p. 89), to set an example, to gain Lady Catherine's approval. His reasons are selfish, but his intention is sound. When he meets Charlotte, someone with equal aims, they marry. Elizabeth is horrified, but the Hunsford visit reveals a marriage that works. Possessions take the place of affection, but it is a stable social unit and therefore valid. Charlotte has a 'degree of contentment' (p. 132) and by the end of the book the couple are expecting a child, fulfilling the purpose of this kind of marriage and offering the couple an established place in society.

The success of Charlotte's marriage begins to change Elizabeth's mind. After Darcy's letter and her self-realization, she matures further. Soon the Wickham she was prepared to marry without money seems 'mercenary' (p. 170) for wanting an unequal match. The superiority in Darcy that once outraged now appeals: 'to be mistress of Pemberley might be something' (p. 201). His doubts about their social inequality now seem more sensible.

Elizabeth still retains her basic belief in marriage based on love rather than practicalities, as when she refuses to agree to Lady Catherine's marriage arrangements, and maintains her right to choose a husband. But she now knows how essential practical considerations are, and when she marries Darcy and moves to the comfort and elegance of Pemberley, she has also achieved an adult view of marriage as a practical and necessary financial contract.

What of the 'impractical' aspects of marriage, sexuality and romance? Jane Austen's view of sexuality seems old-fashioned, even for her day.

There is little examination of the feelings and responses sexual attraction can bring. To Jane Austen sexuality was far less vital to relationships than its counterpart, affection. Once respect, regard and love were established and validated by marriage, which included in it the framework of family and social life, then sexuality was acceptable and taken for granted. Outside marriage, sexuality was merely self-indulgent, and therefore a threat to society.

Mr and Mrs Bennet's marriage, originally based only on 'youth and beauty' (p. 194), ended in contempt because respect and affection had died. Lydia and Wickham's relationship has the same beginnings, but this time outside marriage, beginning with an elopement where 'passions were stronger than . . . virtue' (p. 252). From the very beginning Elizabeth condemns this. It is unconcerned with the effect on family, society, even upon the partnership, and it is totally selfish. The marriage must fail and it does. Elizabeth's judgement is confirmed by Jane Austen, and the marriage fades into indifference.

Elizabeth's view of the sexually based marriage changes little through the course of the book. She at first responds to Wickham's 'beauty . . . countenance . . . figure' (p. 63), but very soon realizes that appearance is not everything. It has to be matched by real worth. She realizes, too, that Darcy's goodness more than compensates for any lack of 'appearance' (p. 185), while he, at first thinking her 'not handsome enough' (p. 13), in the end finds her 'loveliest Elizabeth' (p. 297). Elizabeth also takes a stand against conventional opinion and questions Lydia's marriage. Amidst general rejoicing she alone sees the difference between a physically based marriage and a working relationship. 'For *this* we are to be thankful?' she asks (p. 245). All this shows what Elizabeth and Darcy eventually learn – that obvious physical attraction may mislead, but once affection brings knowledge of and respect for one's partner, true desire follows.

Romance, instantaneous and uncritical admiration of the beloved in a framework of meetings, conversations, dances and flattery, has a firm place in the novel. It is the conventional way to form affectionate marriages. Only Jane and Bingley's relationship is classically romantic, based on 'true affection' (p. 83). They pass through all the stages of romance – attraction, a resolved threat, a proposal followed by happiness. Elizabeth, knowing both to be good people, sees marriage as the 'happiest, wisest, most reasonable end'.

Romance is, however, criticized. Bingley is emotionally weak. He has been 'often . . . in love' (p. 162), and Mrs Gardiner suspects his feelings. The relationship is broken (and later mended) on Darcy's advice, not because of the couple's genuine incompatibility. Their romantic relationship will only work because both are perfectly amiable (p. 280).

Elizabeth begins by favouring romance. She is quickly attracted to Wickham, seeing him as a 'conquest' (p. 76), and begins to view Colonel Fitzwilliam similarly. Nonetheless she is too realistic, and too good a character to maintain this for long. She refuses to flirt where there is no affection, and laughs not only at other people's romances but also at her own. Once she begins to know herself, she realizes the truth about her feelings for Wickham and replaces them with a more realistic and deeper appreciation of Darcy (p. 252).

Darcy must also reconsider his views on marriage in the course of the book. From the start his is a practical outlook. He must learn the place of real affection and replace his concern for Elizabeth's social inferiority with respect for her true character. At first he feels almost emotionally threatened by his romantic impulses. He is 'bewitched' (p. 46), and in 'danger' (p. 51). At the first proposal, it is clear that his emotions need to change. He must learn before marrying Elizabeth that real love is selfless, not self-indulgent, and place romance in its right context just as she must.

Jane Austen obviously sees her heroine's marriage as a model one, the outcome of the novel her readers have been hoping for, and one that rises above the other marriages in the book. What makes it so ideal?

Elizabeth and Darcy's marriage is primarily a sound personal relationship where each person gives something and helps the other to mature. Secondly, the marriage marks a step to this maturity for each of them. By learning to put the other first, they have advanced from the self-centredness of their unmarried lives. They have learnt to accept responsibility for themselves and each other, and to put their relationship in realistic perspective. In Elizabeth's case, this means accepting the importance of marriage as a sound financial and social contract; for both it means realizing that infatuation is not the basis for a lifelong commitment.

Chiefly, however, they have matured by casting aside their main faults – pride and prejudice – through their relationship with each other. This is the real object of love and marriage; not financial security, physical passion or flattering romance, but the self-development that a true relationship brings about. Pride and prejudice, in Elizabeth and Darcy respectively, are combined, and the worst aspects neutralized by an affection that leads inevitably to marriage.

The inner maturing of Elizabeth and Darcy is marked by their marriage. Once adults, the 'proud' Darcy and 'wild' Elizabeth can take their place in society and form a true family.

Parents and Children

Jane Austen's interest in loving relationships and marriage leads her naturally to look at family life. The role of parents and children is therefore an important one in *Pride and Prejudice*.

Like death, the fact of child-bearing is so inevitably a part of life that she hardly mentions it in the novel. 'Adult' parents and children and their influence on each other's lives are examined in great detail.

We might think that parents should be loving, protective and supportive, so it is interesting to notice that the most important parents in *Pride and Prejudice* – and in many other Jane Austen novels – are all to some extent absent, ineffectual or positively damaging. Once more, Jane Austen suggests the necessary attributes of parenthood by their marked absence in this novel.

Mr Bennet, Elizabeth's father, is ineffectual rather than wrong. His main faults are his cynicism and his passivity. His failed marriage has given him a mocking, cynical attitude, particularly towards his wife, so that the girls too have ceased to acknowledge her. Jane Austen strongly condemns 'the disadvantages which must attend the children of so unsuitable a marriage' (p. 194), that lack of marital loyalty which leads to the breakdown of respect within a family.

Mr Bennet's passivity has even more serious consequences. In chapter 41 Elizabeth attempts to persuade her father to act decisively and as a good parent for once. Mr Bennet refuses to take any real responsibility for his children, thinking that if he lets them work out their own salvation, everything will be for the best. In fact, however, as much as he may dislike providing it, Lydia needs a firm hand and good direction.

However, Mr Bennet is probably the best parent in the book. His raising of the girls has at least produced the bright Elizabeth and the improved Jane. He has real affection for these two, though he has difficulty showing it, and he cares enough to visit Bingley, to forbid Elizabeth to marry Collins, and to question her over her love for Darcy in a scene which shows his real concern and understanding of her character. It is Mr Bennet who, of all the family but for Jane, visits Pemberley the most frequently after the marriage.

Elizabeth's mother is a different character entirely, a silly, self-centred woman and a poor parent. Like Lydia, she lacks emotional maturity, and we can see where Elizabeth gets her impulsiveness and lack of rationality. Mrs Bennet's unawareness of financial reality, paralleled by her husband's, causes real problems. Both parents should have thought of the future.

Mrs Bennet tries to compensate for the lack of money in the family by husband-hunting for her daughters. In many ways, her compulsive match-making is funny. It is also wrong. She judges by appearance and wealth with little thought for her daughters' future happiness. So she manipulates Jane, fails to realize the tragedy of Lydia's elopement, and pressures Elizabeth over Collins's proposal: 'I have done with you from this very day' (p. 95). Also notice how her lack of tact and her sense of personal triumph nearly ruin Jane's relationship with Bingley and seem to threaten Elizabeth's with Darcy.

Remember, however, that to a large extent Mrs Bennet's concern is justified. If her husband should die, she and her daughters will be destitute. Also consider that though three of her daughters are 'very silly' (p. 190), two at least are successful.

Lady Catherine de Bourgh is one degree worse than Mrs Bennet. While having the same match-making tendencies, she is both proud and overbearing, and her daughter reflects the poor parental guidance she gives. We see little contact between Lady Catherine and Anne, but the mother obviously dominates and at the same time overprotects the daughter so that she does not develop as she should: 'she would have performed delightfully . . . if her health had allowed' (p. 144). We can also assume, from Lady Anne's behaviour towards everyone, that she has her mother's pride and lack of awareness, a poor inheritance for anyone.

Other parents we see in the book are equally lacking in good qualities. The Lucases happily agree to their daughter's marrying a man 'neither sensible nor agreeable' (p. 103); Wickham has obviously inherited his mother's extravagance; Collins's father was 'illiterate and miserly' (p. 61).

Only Mr and Mrs Gardiner seem to be satisfactory parents. This is shown not so much in their attitude to their own children, but more to Jane and Elizabeth. When Elizabeth needs help, she turns to Mrs Gardiner, who gives her sensible, direct but tactful advice. When Darcy meets and is impressed by the Gardiners at Pemberley, it is as if Elizabeth has introduced him to her real parents. Mr Gardiner takes over effectively from Mr Bennet during the elopement, and the couple marry Lydia from their own house. The Gardiners provide the correct advice, support and love that Elizabeth should have had from her own parents, and it is significant that they assume a key role in the last chapter.

Parents and their roles are obviously shown in *Pride and Prejudice*. Children and their roles are less obviously dealt with. The idea of maturing out of childhood, however, is important. Children mark their maturity by accepting their parents, but also by gaining their independence from them. Surely so many of Jane Austen's parental figures are failures in order that her heroines may more easily mature by themselves.

Of the Bennet girls, there is one prime example of failure in this. Lydia is wilful, shows little real affection and even less respect for her parents. We see this from Elizabeth's and Darcy's criticisms and also from her own behaviour. She has no thought for her parents, or their feelings over the elopement, and completely disregards Mr Bennet's obvious disapproval after the marriage. Almost more serious is her response to those substitute parents, the Gardiners, to whose kindness she is indifferent, even hostile. Lydia gains no insight into any adult's real personality, and whilst gaining her independence through marriage, moves from parents to husband for all the wrong reasons and so learns nothing.

Elizabeth and Jane try to love their parents, though their mother irritates and their father often ignores them. Jane shoulders the burden of Lydia's elopement from her mother, and supports her father on his return from London, but she hardly changes in her attitude towards them.

It is Elizabeth whose view develops the most. As she matures, particularly after Darcy's comments during the proposal and in the letter, she realizes more clearly her parents' faults, that her mother's tactlessness has jeopardized Jane, her father's passivity has endangered Lydia and the family's inferiority probably alienated Darcy for ever. However, she can still forgive and almost forget, bearing with her mother, and not remonstrating with her father when he admits his fault.

In the end, however, she gains her independence. That Elizabeth stands up to her father when he questions her love for Darcy, choosing her husband rather than her family, shows that she has matured enough to follow her own heart, and has gained emotional self-sufficiency even from her beloved father. She now regards Pemberley as her home, Darcy as her 'family' (p. 309), and she is ready to begin the social circle again by becoming a good parent to her own children.

Humour

At first sight, *Pride and Prejudice* may not seem a humorous novel. We do not immediately laugh out loud at the course of events. Nevertheless, once we have learned to appreciate the kind of humour it contains and its reasons for being there, we can see that *Pride and Prejudice* is, in fact, just this sort of book, a social comedy.

Jane Austen's humour pokes fun at people by comparing the way they are with the way they should be. This satire makes us smile rather than laugh at people's faults, and we may also smile, rather ruefully, as we recognize our own faults in theirs.

These faults are not tragic flaws, but ordinary everyday deficiencies: pride and prejudice, vanity, snobbery, hypocrisy, moral blindness. People show these faults by their actions, but more clearly in Jane Austen's work by what they say. She uses the basic dramatic techniques of the Restoration comedies of Manners, adapted for the novel, to reveal people's characters and their flaws in conversation.

The caricatures in *Pride and Prejudice* form obvious targets for satire. They actually represent faults shown in every aspect of their speech and behaviour, so can be criticized easily and obviously.

Mr Collins is a clergyman, a profession supposed to be charitable, Christian and humble. In fact, he is the very opposite. Look, for example, at the way he dominates the conversation at Longbourn, grovels to Lady Catherine in the hope of another living and makes sarcastic comments to Darcy at the Netherfield ball. In particular, look at the way he proposes to Elizabeth in chapter 18. His pompous language, overlong words and too-formal courtesy bring Elizabeth 'so near laughing' (p. 89) that she cannot speak. His reasons for marrying, far from being concerned with the love which should be found in a proposal, are ridiculous because they are so business-like. He cannot help mentioning Elizabeth's lack of dowry – he even knows the exact amount she will inherit. Finally, he cannot accept Elizabeth's refusal, telling her she must marry him. After all, she won't get anyone else!

This is all so removed from the classic proposal that we and Elizabeth have to be amused, but there is a serious message in this. Whilst trying to be the perfect lover, Collins in fact proves himself to be the exact opposite – mercenary, self-centred, condescending. Not only is the scene comic, but it shows what a potential husband – and a clergyman – should *not* do.

Mrs Bennet is comic in a different way. She is not haughty or formal but too obviously lacking in restraint and self-respect. She flaps around trying to manipulate everyone, but in fact is a figure of fun. In the first chapter of the novel, which effectively sets the comic tone for the whole book, we see her trying to persuade Mr Bennet to visit Bingley. The humorous aspect of this scene is that Mrs Bennet is unwittingly the target for her husband's mockery. He pretends ignorance of Bingley, comments that Mrs Bennet is as likely to be courted as the girls, and suggests she pay the visit. She has no idea he is teasing her, playing on her vanity, pretending not to know what she is talking about. We see a silly woman being ridiculed by her intelligent husband, and it is amusing.

What is not so amusing is that, as Jane Austen points out, after twenty-three years of marriage, Mrs Bennet does not understand her husband and has no self-knowledge at all. A marriage that is, on the face of it, successful is in fact very unhappy. Once more, a seemingly humorous scene gives a serious lesson.

Lady Catherine de Bourgh is more powerful than the other comic figures. As a landowner, she should take responsibility for her people and use her power wisely. Instead, she bullies her tenants and uses her position to encourage sycophants like Collins. From the first dinner at Rosings, it is obvious that she wants attention, praise and gratitude. She likes nothing better than to talk 'without any intermission' (p. 136), to pry into other people's business, dictate which games should be played, even decide 'what weather they were to have on the morrow' (p. 139). By such tongue-in-cheek comments Jane Austen points out how Lady Catherine abuses her power.

As with all caricatures, Lady Catherine has a dark side. When she visits Elizabeth at Longbourn to challenge the match with Darcy, though as exaggerated as ever she is no longer comic. She is a real threat.

The main comic figures then, are caricatures of faults. But the more realistic, more important figures in the book are also mocked. Particularly in the first, less serious section up to Darcy's first proposal, Jane Austen loves to point out faults in her hero and heroine.

Darcy's faults are gently highlighted. He is certain (though like Elizabeth, we know the truth) that he has his pride under 'good regulation' (p. 51). He grumpily sniffs that Jane smiles too much and we, like Bingley, smile at him for saying it. He also makes some particularly crushing remarks, aimed at Caroline Bingley, when, for example, she and Elizabeth are walking round the Netherfield drawing room (p. 50).

Elizabeth too is mocked, by the comparison of how she likes to think she is – sensitive, aware, sensible – with what she really is. Her smile at Darcy's comment (p. 51) is amusing because she is guilty of the same fault herself. Her horror at Wickham's tale about Darcy is sadly comic when we realize she is being played like a fish on a hook. Her confident 'one knows exactly what to think' (p. 73) is wryly amusing because her confidence is so totally misplaced.

After Darcy's proposal, however, Jane Austen is less eager to mock her main characters. The business of self-realization is too vital to be satirized.

Which brings us to a word of warning about mockery. Like her father, Elizabeth is said to be amused at 'follies . . . nonsense, whims and inconsistencies' (p. 50); people's stupidity and hypocrisy. Mr Bennet seems a little unkind; he encourages people like Mr Collins and his own wife to make fools of themselves. At first, though, Elizabeth's attitude seems valid, enabling her to laugh at herself as well as others. However, we soon learn that mockery can, without care, be a sly form of self-elevation at others' expense, and can blind us to their good points. Elizabeth claims not to ridicule what is 'wise or good' (p. 50), but she does. She ridicules Darcy in order to show her 'wit' (p. 185). She has to learn not to do this, and by the end of the book, though she still teases Darcy, she does it in a loving, responsible way. Take care, says Jane Austen, to use humour wisely.

You might like to consider, as a way of judging for yourself the humour in *Pride and Prejudice*, what would happen if it were not there. Imagine the book without the satire, the humorous characters, Mr Collins, Lady Catherine and Mrs Bennet. What would it lose in terms of entertainment, contrast, revelation of character and lessons to be learnt? By considering these points, you should be able to decide the place and importance of humour in the novel.

Glossary

Abhorrence: hatred
Ablution: washing
Accede: agree
Accost: address
Acquiescence: agreement
Acquisition: gain
Acrimony: bitterness
Actuate: motivate
Addresses: courtship
Adieu: farewell
Affability: courtesy
Affinity: relationship
Affliction: misery
Agitation: excitement
Alacrity: speed
Allay: lessen
Alliance: union
Allurement: temptation
Amendment: improvement
Animation: liveliness
Antagonist: opponent
Antechamber: room leading to a
    larger one
Apothecary: doctor
Apparel: dress
Approbation: approval
Arch: innocently roguish

Art: skill
Article: contract
Asperity: sharpness
Assembly: ball
Assiduous: persevering
Attain: gain
Attorney: lawyer
Austerity: sternness
Avail: profit, use
Avow: admit
Avowal: admission
Aweful: impressive
Backgammon: a board game
Barouche: four-wheeled carriage
Beaux: admirers
Benificence: active kindness
Bequest: legacy
Blowzy: untidy
Calico: bleached cotton
Cambric: fine linen
Candour: frankness,
    open-mindedness
Canvass: discuss
Capital: the best
Caprice: unaccountable change
Cassino: a card game
Cessation: pause

Chagrin: disappointment

Chaise: an open carriage

Circulation: movement

Circumspection: caution

Cogent: convincing

Commerce: card game

Commiseration: pity

Compass: include

Complacency: satisfaction

Complaisance: deference, politeness

Composition: construction

Conciliate: appease

Concurrence: agreement

Confidante: someone to confide or trust in

Connubial: married

Consequence: rank

Consign: hand over

Constitution: health

Constrain: force

Construe: interpret

Contrariety: opposition

Contrariwise: on the other hand

Contrivance: cunning plan

Contrive: manage, plan

Controvert: dispute

Conversible: able to be talked to

Coquetry: flirtatious behaviour

Cordial: kind

Countenance: encourage, expression, support

Counterpart: equal

Covey: brood of partridges

Curricle: light two-wheeled carriage

Decamp: leave suddenly

Deck: cover

Decorum: correct, polite behaviour

Degradation: lowering

Demean: lower

Denominate: call

Deportment: bearing, manners

Depravity: corruption, viciousness

Depreciate: belittle

Deranged: confused

Descent: ancestry

Design: plan

Destitute: without resources

Devoid: empty of

Diffidence: shyness

Diffuse: spread out

Diminution: diminishing

Disapprobation: disapproval

Discernment: insight

Discomposure: agitation

Discontinuance: ceasing

Discourse: conversation

Discreditable: shameful

Disengaged: detached

Dismission: dismissal

Disposition: character; arrangement

Dissemble: conceal, disguise

Dissipation: frivolous amusement; wasteful spending

Divert: entertain

Draught: medicine

Ductile: easily led, flexible

Eclat: conspicuous success
Effectual: useful
Efficacy: effectiveness
Effusions: unrestrained words
Eminence: hill
Encroach: intrude
Encumbrance: annoyance
Engage: promise
Engagement: contract
Enormity: wickedness
Ensigncy: commission in the
     army
Entail: settlement of inheritance
Epithet: description
Equipage: carriage with horses
     and servants
Equivocal: of double meaning
Establish: firmly believe
Establishment: household
Estimation: judgement
Etiquette: code of polite
     behaviour
Execution: performance
Exertion: action
Exigence: emergency
Expedient: advantageous,
     suitable
Expeditiously: speedily
Expostulation: remonstration
Express: telegram
Extenuate: excuse
Faculty: sense
Felicity: good luck, happiness
First circles: highest rank
Folio: book, page
Forbearance: patience, restraint

Fordyce's sermons: a book of
     serious religious sermons
Formidable: hard to overcome
Fortitude: courage
Foundation: basis
Fretful: worried
Gallantry: courtesy to women
Gamester: gambler
Gaudy: tastelessly showy
Gig: two-wheeled carriage
Going forward: happening
Gratification: pleasure
Hackney coach: horse-drawn
     carriage for hire
Hackneyed: common, overused
Hauteur: haughtiness
Heal the breach: patch up the
     quarrel
Heinous: criminal
High diversion: great amusement
Impetuous: rash
Implacable: unappeasable
Implicit: unspoken
Impolitic: unsuitable, unwise
Importune: bother
Impropriety: indecency
Impunity: no bad results, injury
Impute: attribute
In default of: if there were no
In lieu: instead
Incredulity: disbelief
Indispensable: necessary
Infamous: notorious
Infamy: notorious wickedness
Ingenuity: cleverness
Iniquitous: wicked

Injunction: order

Insensible: unaware

Insensibility: lack of emotion

Insipidity: tastelessness

Intercourse: communication, connection

Intimate: close friend

Intimation: hint

Intolerable: unbearable

Invective: violent verbal attack

Involuntary: unwilling

Irremediable: incurable, unsolvable

Laconic: brief

Laity: laymen not clergy

Lamentation: mournful words

Languor: tiredness

Licentiousness: freedom, lewdness

Livery: uniform worn by servants

Living: salaried post given to a clergyman often under the control of the local landowner

Loo: card game

Lottery tickets: game of chance

Magnitude: importance

Manifold: many

Material: real

Mien: air

Mode: way

Mollify: appease

Morality: ethics, points of behaviour

Mortification: humiliation

Mortify: humiliate

Muslin: delicate cotton

Nuptials: wedding celebrations

Obeisance: respectful gesture

Office: job

Officiousness: intrusive, meddling behaviour

Oppressive: overwhelming

Overset: overturned, upset

Overture: offer

Palatable: pleasing

Pales: fence

Palliation: alleviation

Paltry: petty

Panegyric: praise

Partiality: bias, fondness

Pathetic: unhappy

Pecuniary: financial

Pedantic: bookish, formal

Perusal: thorough reading

Perverseness: error

Petition: request

Phaeton: four-wheeled open carriage

Picturesque: like a picture

Piquet: card game for two

Pliancy: flexibility

Policy: craftiness

Postilion: person who rides on one of the horses drawing a carriage when there is no driver

Precipitance: hurried action

Preface: introduce

Preferment: promotion

Premise: basis

Prepossession: favourable
    prejudice
Preservative: safety
Pretension: claim
Prevail: persuade
Probity: honesty
Profligate: extravagant, immoral
Prognostic: foreboding, warning
Propensity: inclination
Propitious: favourable
Propriety: right behaviour,
    rightfulness
Prudence: caution, discretion,
    wisdom
Prudential: wise
Purport: meaning
Quadrille: card game for four
    couples
Quickness: awareness,
    intelligence, speed
Ragoût: spiced meat and
    vegetable stew
Rapacity: keenness
Reanimate: enliven again
Receipt, on the: on receiving
Rectitude: rightness
Redress: reparation
Regimentals: uniform
Rencontre: meeting
Repair: go
Repine: fret
Reprehensible: blameworthy
Reproof: blame, rebuke
Repugnance: disgust
Requisite: needed
Reserve: restraint

Revive: restore
Revolution: change
Sally: rush out
Sanction: authorize
Sanguine: confident
Saucy: cheeky
Scrupulous: conscientious
Self-complacency:
    self-satisfaction
Self-consequence: self-importance
Se'night: week (seven nights)
Sensibility: capacity to feel,
    sensitivity
Servility: slavishness
Set-down: put-down
Settlement: legal provision
Simper: smile artificially
Smirk: smile stupidly
Solicit: invite
Solicitation: request
Solicitude: worry
Spar: crystalline material –
    Derbyshire is known for
    its rock caves
Spleen: spite
Stamp: kind
Station: place
Steadfast: constant, firm
Stricture: critical remark
Subsist: exist
Suit: request
Superintend: look after, manage
Surmise: doubtful guess
Susceptibility: ability to be
    affected
Synonymous: with the same

meaning but in different context

Tacit: unspoken

Tenor: tone

Tête à tête: private conversation

Threadbare: overused, well-worn

Too unassailed: not influenced enough

Tractable: easily handled

Transaction: piece of business

Transition: change

Transports: strong emotions

Trifle with: refuse to take seriously

Turnpike: toll-gate

Turn the tide of: alter, change

Tythe: tax to support the clergy

Unalloyed: untaxed

Ungovernable: uncontrollable

Unshackle: untie

Unstudied: unaffected, unintentional

Untinctured: uncoloured

Vent: outlet

Venture: try

Verdure: greenery

Vestibule: hall, lobby

Vexatious: annoying

Vindication: proving the rightness of someone's actions

Vingt-et-un: card game

Violation: infringement

Vogue: fashion

Vouchsafe: condescend

Wanton: irresponsible

Whimsical: unpredictable

Discussion Topics and Examination Questions

Your understanding and appreciation of the novel will be much increased if you discuss aspects of it with other people. Here are some of the topics you can consider:

1. How far do you think that *Pride and Prejudice* is the best title for the novel? What evidence do you find to support Jane Austen's original choice of title, *First Impressions*?

2. Which incident in the novel do you find most dramatic and why?

3. Do you have any sympathy for Mr Collins and Lady Catherine de Bourgh? If not, why not?

4. Discuss the part played by letters in *Pride and Prejudice*.

5. Select three or four scenes from the novel and try, through discussion, to bring out the main aspects of the comedy in *Pride and Prejudice*.

6. Is it true that Elizabeth dominates the novel? Make out a case for considering any other character or characters just as important.

7. What have you learned about Jane Austen's society from *Pride and Prejudice*?

8. Discuss the view that Jane and Bingley are uninteresting, whereas the reader responds to Lydia and Wickham despite their faults.

9. Select three or four conversations in the novel. In what ways is Jane Austen's dialogue true to life?

10. 'She is more concerned with money and property than anything else.' How far would you consider this a fair comment on *Pride and Prejudice*?

11. 'Right behaviour and right judgement, these are Jane Austen's concerns in *Pride and Prejudice*.' Discuss.

12. Discuss the presentation of marriage through contrast as seen in the Bennets and the Gardiners.

13. 'There is too much talk, too little action.' How far would you agree with this assessment of *Pride and Prejudice*?

14. Do you find the changes in Elizabeth and Darcy convincing in view of their earlier pride and prejudice?

15. Discuss any aspect of the novel not mentioned above – for example, snobbery, family life, the position of the girls and their need to marry, or any of the minor characters and what you think they represent.

The Examination

You may find that the set texts chosen by your teacher have been selected from a very wide list of suggestions in the examination syllabus. The questions in the examination paper will therefore be applicable to many different books. Here are some possible questions which you could answer by making use of *Pride and Prejudice*:

1. Write an account of any character in a novel or story you have read who appears to be proud, arrogant and objectionable, but is later shown to have good qualities.

2. Using one of your set books, show what picture of life at a particular historical time is given.

3. Write about the presentation of a family in any book you have read closely.

4. Write a description of a character in your chosen book who is unconsciously funny and unsympathetic at the same time.

5. Choose a scene from the book you are studying which is dramatic and moving. Say how it affects the plot of the book.

6. What part do secrets play in your chosen book? Show how they influence the actions of any of the characters.

7. What use is made of contrast in your chosen book? Write about any two characters or situations in which contrast is an important element.

8. Write about the development of any relationship in the book you are studying.

9. In what ways is a sudden or unexpected situation or occurrence used in the novel or story you are studying?

10. For which character in your chosen book do you feel most sympathy and why?

11. What are the main social concerns in a novel you are studying? Choose any two – from, say, snobbery, career, status, the importance of money, living conditions, etc. – and examine them closely.

12. What part does misunderstanding play in your set book? You should refer to one or two important instances of it in the story and show what effect it has on a character or characters.

13. Write about the difference between what appears and what actually is in your chosen book (i.e. how characters behave compared with what they really are).

14. What do you learn of *the author's* attitudes in any book you have studied closely.

15. Write about the position or role of the main female character in your chosen book.